DIRTY SOUTH

BY WANDA M. COPPEDGE

Cover illustration by Tyrelle Smith

ISBN 978-1-943515-83-7

For Momma and Daddy

Acknowledgments

I would like to thank my mother, who's my number-one fan: for reading and rereading....and rereading this book. For her continuous encouragement whenever I was feeling discouraged. And my daughters, Keita and Nia, for their undying support, because I'm their mother. I would also like to thank my sister, Jennifer, who was sensitive enough to my passion and introduced me to the best publishing company in the world, AcuteByDesign.

And, of course, AcuteByDesign, especially Michel, for taking a chance on a twelve-year-old dream and making it a reality. Also, Cyn, the sharpest editor on this planet, and Tyrelle, an amazing illustrator, for their special attention to the book.

And my Master and friend, the Lord Jesus Christ, for preserving me for my purpose.

Thank you!

AcuteByDesign is a teeny, tiny book publishing
company with a big mission:

To produce and publish high quality diverse,
multicultural, and socially relevant
books for children and young readers;
their teachers, and parents

To provide opportunities for teachers and
under-represented writers and illustrators to
publish their dream book, and

To provide small grants to teachers and
parent associations to help provide resources
for underserved students and classrooms.

Thank you for helping to make that dream
come true for so many!

www.acutebydesign.com

Weeping, dirty South
With blood on its mouth

MISSISSIPPI 1955

The day was young. The willow trees hung low and wide, draping the bank along the stream—like fingertips dipping in the stream's end. The grass seemed extra green that day. The mockingbird spoke up with its artificial voice—a hummingbird, the rustling trees, chattering stream, the whirling wind. The sky was decidedly blue—untainted with clouds. Every living thing that God had created was on its best behavior, except for man. Man was not on his best behavior. Man had become tainted by the lies of history, giving mental credence that one human race, namely, the white race was better than the other, subjugating the black race.

For hundreds of years we had been used as stepping stones, whipping posts—beaten down like animals. Dismissed like the first breath, then the second, then the third breath, and so on. No thought of what it took to breathe; how hard the lungs must work to keep the breathing organic, without full comprehension that without them, we will surely die. Surly their actions are toward the black race. But what have we done? What had the black man done but be black? What had the black woman done but be black? The hate and the ridiculing and the derogatory name-calling: *Spook, Coon, Bugaboo, Spade, Nigger, Nigger, Nigger!*

They beat me 'til I fell unconscious; and in between my coming to, I thought of the people who mattered the most to me-- my mom and dad, my sisters, and of course, my sweet Maybelle. I knew she couldn't have said such things. I knew she couldn't have said that I...well, it don't matter now. I'm beaten to a bloody pulp, unrecognizable to the human eye.

This is the dirty South, and these are our stories....

Tiger was born and raised in the time of Crow Mississippi, where lynching still ruled as the source of punishment, and every black person in the South feared for his or her life. He feared for his life that night. He didn't know what to expect—well, he did...just not to what degree. He always wondered, but he never thought that it would happen to him.

You see, he met her at the store off-road on the way home. She was so beautiful. Her name was Maybelle.   He called her Bell, for short. She had flaxen blonde hair, just brushing her shoulders—downy and smooth. He used to love when it kissed against her slightly sunburnt skin. He fell hard for her. He didn't know why he chose her. Maybe it was the fact that he couldn't, and that those old Crow laws said he couldn't. But whatever the case, he fell for the bait, the trap that white men wait to hang a black man for. And she fell for him, too, or so it seemed....

"Tiger, go on down to that store and tell your father to come on home. It's gettin' late."

"Yes, ma'am."

Tiger was ten years old when it happened, when he witnessed two dead men in his father's store, poolin' in each other's blood. He couldn't believe his eyes. His mother sent him to go to the store that his father inherited from *his* father. His mother always sent Tiger to the store to fetch his dad whenever she thought he was workin' too late. I guess in the greater scheme, she feared what might happen to him being out so late at night. "Them whities are crazy," she'd say constantly, and then sent Tiger right out to fetch him home. The store sat off-road, where a bunch of trees and dirt resided. His dad's store was most popular with the more impoverished families: sharecroppers and domestic workers. They would always come to him because they knew that he'd catch'em a break when they was low on cash. He was just like that. Tiger's mom, however, would fuss at him—saying, how could he make a profit if he kept doing favors for folk, which was why she took on a job teaching the Negro children at the school up the road from where they lived.

Night fell hard by the time Tiger arrived at the store. It felt strange. He couldn't quite explain it—like he was walkin' into somethin'—and his instincts were right. The trail of blood stopped him in his tracks. It led right up the stairs and inside of the store. He was confused and frightened. Questions rose rapidly through his head. Was he dead? Was the man he looked up to no longer alive?

The door was cracked. He stood in front of the store for what seemed like hours. Finally, he made his way up the stairs, allowing the bloody trail to guide him. He pushed the door wider with his right hand, shaking. He looked around the store, and things were spilled everywhere, as if a scuffle had taken place. He looked down and was standing in a puddle of blood. Without thinking, he jumped and immediately yelled for his dad. He didn't answer, so he dashed toward the back of the store, at the same time, in fear of what he might find. And that's when he saw the two dead men. There was so much blood that he couldn't tell who was bleeding more. Even the color seemed different. Like one man's blood looked lighter than the other man's. Or maybe it was the way the moon shone on one of them. Nonetheless, he was entranced to see one a scarlet color and the other a deep burgundy. His eyes trailed to his father, leaning against the wall. His shirt was all bloody, while the shotgun he held in his right hand lay slightly on his inner right thigh. He appeared to be out of breath—or maybe just scared, like Tiger.

"Get a bag and some rope."

He broke Tiger's thought.

"What happened, Dad?"

"Hurry up, boy, and stop askin' questions."

Tiger quickly obliged his order. Their bodies were heavy. Tiger wondered why, but dared not ask. They tied the men up, his father carrying most of the weight, and dragged them to the back of the store.

"What we gonna do wit'em dad?"

"We gonna bury these sumbitches behind the wall."

Tiger's brain was wrecked by now. *Behind the wall?* "How are we gonna do that?" He thought he'd said it to himself, but then he looked up and saw his father looking straight at him.

"Boy, quit askin' questions and follow my lead."

And he did. They got the cement and mixed it. His dad had some bricks from the last job he did, when they both built an addition on to the store.

"Hand me them bricks, Tiger."

His father had taught him to lay bricks, a trade that he insisted that he learn. "Ray," his father counseled, "you'll never know when you're gonna need this trade, so learn it like you're gonna build homes for a hundred families." So instead of him using the trade to build homes for families, he used it to build an addition to his store and to put up a second wall to bury two dead men behind it.

Tiger continued following his father's lead, mixing the cement and laying the bricks; and by dawn, the two men who had intruded his father's workspace and were shot—one twice in the chest, and the other twice in the back—were securely buried behind the newly built wall in the back of the store. Afterward, they cleaned up the place and scrubbed the floor. By 8 a.m., the store was opened for business. He never told his father this, but he felt a mysterious bond with him that night, as if they shared something that his two sisters—and anyone else, for that matter—would never share. No, it wasn't butterflies and daisies, but it was a moment. One he'd never forget.

2

Twice a week, Tiger's mother sent him and his sisters to Mrs. Robinson's house to see about her. Tiger's mother felt she owed that to her since she was the one who killed one of the men that night at the store. Mrs. Robinson wasn't much—just a feeble old woman who had nothing better to do than to sit at her window and watch the world go by. Her husband had left her years ago for being barren. He felt that she was cursed and no longer wanted to be married to her. But little did he know that she fixed her body to not have children. She hated him. He verbally abused her at every turn, and she was sick to death of it. So, she began drinking some kind of concoction her sister sent her from Louisiana.

Her sister was a practicing witch doctor and believed that anything could be remedied with potions and incantations. When her husband asked her what she was drinking, she simply replied, "This will make me a new woman." Her husband patiently waited around for this new woman to appear, but instead got a woman who was prematurely aging and losing her eyesight. He finally left her and married one of the younger girls around town. Eventually, Mrs. Robinson stayed in altogether. Instead, she sat by the window, glaring out at an aging tree with a slight semblance of beauty. Although her sight grew faint, she could still, however, make out shadows; and the closer she got to the object, she was quite sure that she could make out whatever it was that was in her view, dead-on. Ray swore by her. And as far as he was concerned, she was an angel sent by God.

It turned out that she witnessed the two men breaking into the store. Her house sat about twenty yards from the store, and every now and then she'd advised Ray to lock up when he'd stay late. "You got a family. Pay attention," she'd say. He heard but never heeded. He just thought that she was just being old and protective. Besides, how could she tell what was going on, being half-blind and all?

Mrs. Robinson dragged herself out of her house, carrying a shotgun. Ray was scuffling with the one while the other made his way from out of the bushes. He managed to push the one he was fighting down the stairs and immediately ran into the store to grab his shotgun. The one he was fighting got up off the ground, pulled out his gun, and ran in the store behind him. More scuffling went on, and then a shot, and then another. The other one was making his way into the store until Mrs. Robinson stopped him with two gunshots in the back. The man dropped liked a cypress tree on the stairs of the store. Ray ran out of the store and saw a dead man on the steps and Mrs. Robinson holding a shotgun. He stared at her amazed. He didn't know there was a second one and also had no idea that Mrs. Robinson was a good shot.

"You know a trade?"

"What?"

"You know a trade? Layin' bricks, Plasterin'…burying the dead?"

"Uh…brick-layin', I guess?"

"Good. Use it and get dem sumbitches outta here fo' you hung 'fore daylight. Especially for dat ofay layin' dead in yo store." She dragged herself away with her shotgun slung over one shoulder.

"Yes, ma'am."

Ray was shaking all over. He couldn't pull himself together. He threw up on the landing and plopped down on the threshold between the store and the landing. He put his head between his legs. When he found himself collected, he noticed the dead man Mrs. Robinson put two holes through. He didn't recognize him; however, he noticed that he resembled his little brother, who died at the hands of some white men long ago. He also noticed that the dead man wasn't a man at all. "He's just a kid," he said, and a tear welled in his right eye. He snapped out of it and remembered what he had to do. He pulled the young boy into the store, staring at the thick blood that oozed out of him. That was when Tiger arrived.

3

Tiger stopped dead in his tracks. She appeared out of nowhere. Her beauty was intrusive. Not in a bad way, but more in a way that caught a fellow off-guard. Her movements were precise, as if she knew she was being watched. And each movement accentuated her curvaceous build, which he found would lure him into a subjective trance. She was like a Degas painting: graceful porcelain girls, stretching and waiting in their ballet stance. She leaned her body against the doorway of the store, blocking anyone's view. Tiger stared at her and knew he was. She saw him staring and seemed to tease him even more. Tiger found himself not turning away, but rather staring without fear.

"Hey."

He looked over his shoulder as if she were speaking to someone else.

"Me?" He pointed to his chest.

"Yes, you, silly. How are you?"

"I'm all right." He was a bit hesitant but boldly continued the conversation with the girl who could change his life forever. "And you?" Tiger looked shocked. He'd never held a conversation with a white girl before. Surely, he didn't understand the nerve, but he continued on with it.

"You live 'round here?"

"Well, actually, I live up the road." He pointed.

"Oh."

"You know, I walk up and down this road a lot, and I've never seen you before."

"I'm from up north. New Jersey. I'm here for the summer, helping my uncle at the store." She leaned her hip on the doorway and ran her fingers through her flaxen blonde hair. She then caught her fingertip in her hair and began twirling it around and around and around. Tiger couldn't help but notice this entranced gesture of flirtation and smiled to himself.

"Uh...up north? I've always wanted to go. What's it like?"

"Well, not like here...what's with everyone around here?"

"How do you mean?"

"I mean, everyone's afraid of talkin'. How 'bout you? Are you afraid of talkin'?"

"Dependin' who I'm talkin' to."

"Hmmm...You afraid of talkin' to me?"

She cocked her head to one side, and the wind blew her hair back, showing her elongated neck.

"Oddly, no."

"Well, good."

"What's your..."

"Maybelle, who you talkin' to?"

"Nobody, Uncle."

"Well, come on in here and count these preserves, hear?"

"Yes, sir."

She looked at him and waved goodbye. Tiger waved back and slowly ventured his way up the road. He wanted to see her again, to be in her company for a spell. She seemed so easygoing, which made him wonder was everyone from up north like her? Carefree.

"I don't know what's gotten into you, but down here we don't indulge in the Coloreds the way you doin'."

"Why, whatever do you mean, Uncle?" Maybelle crooned in her best southern drawl.

"Don't you get sassy wit' me, gal. You know what I'm speakin'? Didn't yo momma ever tell you what the deal was 'round these parts?"

"Yeah, yeah." She waved him off as if to wave a fly.

Bill leaped across the counter and grabbed her wrist.

"Hey!" she said, surprised.

"Don't you go wavin' me off like I'm nothin'. I know what I'm talkin' 'bout. You can get that Nigger in some serious trouble, you keep messin' 'round the way you doin'."

"My God, what kind of language is that'? My mother never..."

"Well, yo momma done forgot, which is crazy 'cause she was the one who..."

Maybelle's face got tight, and then she hung her head.

"I...I'm sorry. Just stay away from him, hear?"

"Fine."

>>>

Before Tiger's daily check in on Mrs. Robinson, he'd stop by to see his dad. Tiger's dad hadn't been home in a while because the parents had a falling out. However, Tiger made it his business to see him and to update him on the goings on at the household.

"What's the word, Thunderbird?" Ray called out joyously, watching Tiger walk up the road.

"Hey Dad, you need help with that?"

"Naw, son, I got it. Why don't you reach in the drinkbox and get us a couple of drinks."

"Sure, Dad."

They made themselves comfortable—Ray on the top stair, while Tiger took his rightful place on the stair just below him. There was a relaxed silence between them.

Ray noticed the scenery that surrounded them, and began.

"I love Mississippi," he said, taking a swig of his soda.

"Yeah, Dad?"

"Yeah, Son. I do."

"Why? It's just a bunch of dirt and trees; nothin' to this place. I can't wait to leave. White folks so damned nasty..."

"You keep a civil tongue in your mouth, boy. I don't care how old you are. You think Mississippi is the only place where white folks is nasty? Besides, there's still some good 'round here." He leaned back with both elbows bracing himself, while lightly gripping his soda in his left hand. "Sometimes, I just look out here at these willow trees and think about the goodness of God. He made these trees— the way the leaves just swoop down, barely touchin' the ground."

Tiger looked over the horizon, trying to picture what his father saw. Ray continued. "You know, my father almost lost this store."

Really?"

"Yeah, so before he lost it, he sold it to a white man he grew up with. Bud was his name. My father's grandmammy used to clean his family's house, and my dad and Bud used to play together, whenever she would clean their home. They grew to really love one another—like they was blood. They used to call each other brothers. One day, Bud enlisted in the army and when my dad found out, he enlisted too! They fought side by side. My dad even saved his life. And even when they got older they still found a genuine bond for one another. They continued to keep in touch from time to time. Later, my dad purchased some land with the money he made doing odd jobs and built this store by himself. He was twenty-two."

"Wow, dad. I never knew that."

"Well, as time passed, he got in a lot of debt and holdin' a store became too much for him and he was goin' under."

"So what happened?"

"He thought about selling the store but instead of selling it to a total stranger, he decided to get in touch with the same friend, shared his dilemma, and told him that he wanted to sign the store over to him. My dad told him that he'd run it and do odd jobs, and then later buy it back when his debts was cleared."

"Well...couldn't his friend just loan him the money? I mean, they were close, right?"

"My dad didn't want any handouts. He wanted to do it his way or no way at all. He said that he'd lose the store before he took money from anybody. It took him three years to buy it back."

"Three years? Anything could have happened in three years. What if he didn't want to sell the store?

"Yeah, and what if my dad had died tryin'? What if your momma wouldn't have taken a chance on me? What if the breeze didn't blow at its right time? My point, Tiger, is that you gotta learn to trust and take a whole lot of chances. You gotta learn to depend. My father took the chance and trusted somebody he hadn't seen in almost ten years, and if he'd just given up, we wouldn't be sittin' on these steps today, enjoying these drinks."

A slight pause grew between them, and then Tiger asked.

"So, do you trust Momma?"

"I don't wanna talk about your momma right now, Tiger."

"Dad, she misses you. She wants to talk."

"Tiger please, I don't wanna discuss this issue right now. Besides, she's made her choice a long time ago. She don't want nobody like me. She'd rather have somebody smarter. I can't get hurt anymore. She done made her choice a long time ago."

"You're such a hypocrite. Here, you're talkin' about your father trustin' some white man and how things turned out for the better because of it. Now you can't even trust your wife?

"Tiger?!"

"Sir?!"

They stared at each other. "You just don't get it, do you?"

"I get it plenty. I'm not ten anymore, Dad. You just can't pat me on the head and tell me to go play. I'm seventeen years old. I'm gonna fall in love one day, and I need to know that it works."

"What works?"

"Love."

The pause grew heavier this time— only the sound of the wind rustling the leaves, its boldness to be heard.

"Take them bag of groceries to Mrs. Robinson." He tossed the half-empty bottle of his soda in the garbage and made his way toward the inside of the store. Before his left foot crossed the threshold, he turned and looked at Tiger once more. His eyes dropped to the ground. "I still love your momma. I never gave up on her. She gave up on me." His eyes dropped. "Tell your sisters to stop by the store and get these jars of honey. You know how your momma likes..."

His voice trailed. And with that, he walked into the store. Tiger refused to respond. Ray wanted to reach out and grab him, but he couldn't bring himself to do it. He knew Tiger was hurting, but so was he.

"Sure, Dad," he said to himself.

4

Anchorman: So Dr. King, what do you propose to be the outcome of this bus boycott situation?

Dr. King: Well, what the Negro people want is to be treated as equal when riding the buses. We believe that when one pays the same fare, one should be able to ride without any stipulations on where one should sit.

Anchorman: It seems that thus far, you're having a difficult time with the courts regarding your demands.

Dr. King: Yes, but I believe that the tenacity of the Negro people will overshadow the courts' decision. Furthermore, it is our Constitutional right to be treated civil amongst the white race. You see...

Maybelle was on the bed, listening to the interview. As her interest grew, she leaned over and turned up the radio a bit more. While listening, her thoughts went to this afternoon with her forbidden encounter. He was different, all right, she thought. She'd never met anyone quite like him. All the guys up north have a different feel to them, even the Negroes, as if they're too cool or something. But this one seemed genuine.

As her curiosity rose, her thoughts trailed to his slender, dark body, and the way his fingers wiped his brow every time he'd ask her a question. Unknowingly, a smile eased the corners of her mouth. Then she felt a hard sting across her face, throwing her clear off the bed and onto the floor. When she got up, blood was on her bottom lip. She held her face to see who had delivered the blow. It was her Auntie Rose.

"You whore!" She spat out the words. "How could you entertain such a thing?"

"Auntie Rose, what are you talking about?"

"You damn well know what I'm discussin'. Your uncle called me and told me what you was up to. He said that you was outside the store entertainin' conversation with a Negro boy? How you was swoonin' over him? I don't know what y'all are used to up north, but down here, these Niggers need to know their place. We are good Christian folk, and as such, we must obey the laws of the South.

Maybelle couldn't believe what she was hearing. She'd heard about the harsh treatment that Negroes were getting, but to see it first-hand?

"I...I...didn't know...I'm sorry."

"Damn right you are. You will not make a public display outta this family. I don't care who you are!"

"All right..."

"What did you say?"

"I said, all right!"

"You bet it's all right. Now clean yourself up 'fore you get blood on my new carpet...whore."

She touched her face and winced lightly. She grabbed a mirror off of the dresser and inspected the bruise on her bottom lip. She was angry. She thought about her mother and longed for home.

Sure there was racism up north, but not to such a degree as this. This was new to her. She felt everything closing in. She quickly got to her feet and opened the bedroom window. She swung her right leg over the ledge, followed by her left leg, and shimmied down the vines that intertwined each other, which made a ladder for climbing up or down. When she reached the bottom, she cut across the quarter-acre field and onto the wooded path that, hopefully, led to her sanity.

>>>

"Mrs. Robinson? Mrs. Robinson?"

Tiger opened the door to the dimly lit home, hoping not to stumble on or against anything.

"In here," she responded. "Jus' put dat stuff down dere and hep me into da kitchen."

"Yes ma'am." When he entered farther into the house, it was as if he had entered a dark and clammy cave. She desired only natural light, and when evening eclipsed its way through, she lit a candle and walked around with it from room to room. He often wondered why she didn't just turn on her lights, especially when company came. But then he gathered himself and just wanted to get the chore over with as quickly as he could.

"You wanna eat somethin'?" she asked.

"I'm all right, ma'am. Where do you want these bags?"

"Jus' set 'em right dere. You in some kinda hurry, Tiger?"

"I gotta be gettin' home to do my homework."

"Homework," she said to herself. "I was never really much for schoolin' myself. Only a third-grade education. I figure, a Negro like me would end up scrubbin' somebody's floor or pickin' somebody's cotton anyhow."

"Yes, ma'am."

Her inquisitive posture was captured by the fainting sun. Tiger watched her slowly lean in. "Now, I've been knowin' you since you was a bitty thing. You eyein' a gal jus' yet?"

"Well..." He started to share, but decided against it, afraid of what her reaction might be.

"Now don't be 'shamed. I'm plenty interested." Her voice dropped to ease his shyness. It worked, sort of. "Why I been knowin' you since you was a bitty thing. I'm plenty interested."

He still felt apprehensive, and busied himself by putting the canned goods in the cabinet. Mrs. Robinson watched him struggle to put things away because of the little light that was provided in her home. *Why doesn't she cut on a light?!* he thought.

"It's that new girl, Maybelle Clemens, ain't it?"

Tiger paused; but then he continued putting the groceries away. "Well, that's the last of it." He tried to ignore her, but at the same time was baffled as to how she knew who was occupying his thoughts. He'd come to the conclusion that Mrs. Robinson was a half-blind psychic with a hell of a trigger.

She continued, "I understand that you may not wanna talk about it, but I jus' might be the only person who is willin' to listen and won't judge you 'bout it neither. Perhaps give you somethin' to go on?"

He turned to her and slowly slid into the chair at the kitchen table across from her.

"Well, when I saw her... It was somethin' about her. Like I was drawn to her like a magnet. I mean, how could that be? I just saw her today. It's like my whole body went numb. Like she didn't see me as being a Negro, but she saw me as just a man. I think I want to try gettin' to know her a bit more—"

"Well that can't be if'n you don't want your days on this earth cut short." Her voice transcended, as if she'd forgotten he was there, "Yes, we oughta be free to love who we want." Suddenly, her eyes shifted to meet his."You jus' be careful. I'm not gonna tell you dat it can't be done, but you betta be ready for the consequences...if'n you decides to pursue. You know, the South ain't ready for dat kinda love."

Tiger was grateful. He rose from the table and walked toward the door. When he opened it, the sun shone on his face. It relieved some of the anxiety that had overtaken him while he sat at Mrs. Robinson's kitchen table. As he walked down the dirt road, his thoughts streamed to the conversation he'd had with his father earlier. That thought carried him all the way home to greet his mom and his two sisters, and another fatherless supper.

5

Everyone knew that William and Roseanne were meant to be. "A match made in heaven," is what they said. When Bill first saw Roseanne—"Rose" is what he called her because of her strawberry blonde hair, that also smelled of roses—he knew that they would marry. He saw her at a church outing. He was nineteen at the time, and she was only fifteen. Her parents were very protective of their Roseanne and wanted the best for her. The Clemenses moved from Georgia and had been in Mississippi for only a week. The Clemenses also had a younger daughter, Chloe; however, Roseanne was their prize daughter. Her fair skin and slender build caused her to be the talk of Georgia. She followed in her mother's footsteps in pageants, southern etiquette, and such. She was her mother's spitting image. But Chloe was the complete antithesis of what her mother longed for in her two daughters.

Chloe, it seemed, was born to rebel. She never seemed to follow any of the rules that her mother set for her. "Damn it, Chloe! Why do you always defy me?!"her mother always yelled. She knew that this one would be different, even while she was pregnant. She couldn't get any sleep the whole time Chloe was inside of her. "This one's gonna be somethin'," she'd constantly say to herself.

While Roseanne was entered in pageants and etiquette classes, Chloe refused and instead, would sneak out and hide under a tree, reading Dickinson or Whitman. Her mood was as dark as her hair. Sometimes in her quiet time, she pretended that she belonged to another family; one that was free-spirited and didn't care about being perfect because she knew that she wasn't. She didn't have the perfect height, the perfect build, or the perfect skin. So she felt it was no use to try to act perfect, which is why those etiquette classes and pageantries did nothing for her.

Chloe confirmed her waywardness when she decided to help the Coloreds clear the tables at the exclusive country club the Clemenses belonged to in Georgia. The ladies made their way outside and sat on the porch, fanning themselves, while indulging in light refreshments and congenial conversation. The men, however, enjoyed brute banter while smoking cigars in the billiard room. Roseanne sat alongside her mother, just as the other girls did, but Chloe was nowhere to be found. Her mother looked around a few times and through the window, saw her daughter helping the Coloreds clear the dishes, while entertaining in idle conversations.

She was ten at the time. She'd always harbored a certain compassion for those whose rights were being obstructed. Her mother looked up long enough from her brioche and mint julep tea to find her malevolent daughter behaving in the most benevolent way. Mortified, she stormed inside and grabbed her daughter by the arm. Chloe was dragged five blocks by her mother until they were at the front door of their colonial home. She was stunned by her mother's strength. The feet attached to her ten-year old, sixty-pound body barely touched the ground.

Chloe's mother didn't stop there. She continued dragging her daughter, up the stairs and down the hall to her bedroom. Chloe screamed and cried, while her mother pushed her down on the post of Chloe's bed and stripped off her clothes. Afterward, she left the room and returned with a rope in one hand and a leather switch in the other.

"No!" Chloe screamed. She knew what was coming. She tried fighting her off, but her mother was stronger. She grabbed both her arms together and tied them up like a cowboy wrestling cattle. Chloe turned as red as a pepper, enraged and horrified. Her mother tied the remaining rope to the bedpost. She tied it so tight that Chloe lost all feeling in her hands. She grabbed the leather switch and beat her mercilessly on her back where the old scars and most recent scars resided. When she was through, she got down on one knee and glared into Chloe's eyes. "If you want to act like a Nigger, then I'll treat you like one. The next time you feel the need to humiliate me, I'll kill you myself." She released the rope from the post, and Chloe dropped to the floor. Chloe was left there, bloody and scarred.

>>>

"You sure are pretty." Bill said to Roseanne as he leaned into her. "Do you think we can go somewhere and talk? You know, get to know each other better?"

"Why, we are talkin' right now," Roseanne crooned.

"Gal, you know what I mean—without them pryin' eyes." He gestured his eyes toward her father, who was staring right at them.

"Well, I don't know. My father..."

"Roseanne?" Her father cried. Then he waved his hand for her to come to him.

"I gotta go."

"Well, hold on now. When can I see you again? I mean, can I call on you sometime?"

"I...I don't know. I gotta ask my mom and dad."

Her father continued his brazen stare, "Roseanne Clemens, get over here!"

"Roseanne Clemens." Bill repeated. "That sure is a pretty name."

"What's your name?"

"William Simms, but folk 'round here call me Bill."

"Okay, Bill." She smiled at him and then in a low voice, "You can come and call on me some time," and then ran over to her father.

"I surely will, Miss. Roseanne...Simms. I surely will." He said to himself.

>>>

As time passed, Bill and Roseanne were inseparable. Roseanne's father was so impressed with Bill that he gave him a job at the mill where he was head foreman. Bill and Roseanne went out every Saturday night, and he ate at their house every Sunday after church. He had courted her for two years when Bill finally asked for her hand in marriage, with the permission of her father, of course. Roseanne's father was for it, but her mother wanted her to wait at least another year. By then, she'd be eighteen, and would have graduated from finishing school.

"Mrs. Clemens, I don't think I can wait that long. I love her so much. I want her to be mine so that we can begin our life together."

"Well, if you love her that much, what's another year, huh?"

Bill obliged her wish. One evening after supper, Chloe announced that after high school, she would be moving to New York City.

"There's this place called Harlem where a lot of artists reside. I want to be a part of that!"

"Have you completely lost what sense you have left?" her mother responded angrily.

"No. And you can stop demanding me to go to that school Roseanne's in."

"It's a good school. It helps you become a lady. It's congenial."

"Bullshit! It's a bunch of desperate girls trying to get a husband. Charm my ass..."

"How dare you speak to me that way?!"

"You keep a civil tongue in your mouth when you talk to your mother, Chloe," her father chimed in.

"Do you purposefully wake up in the morning and give your father and me hell?" What in God's name are you gonna do in New York City?"

"I want to be a writer. I want to experience other races—."

"You mean the Negro race?" Roseanne interrupted.

"And what if I do? Is there anything wrong with that?" Chloe fought back.

"Why?!" Her mother was exasperated. She couldn't believe what she was hearing. She knew her daughter was odd and disobedient, but this just took all. Was she deliberately trying to hurt her—to dig a hole in her heart?

"There's nothing for me here. I just don't like the South. I hate what it represents." Chloe looked up toward the open sky. "I know there are other things going on in the world, other ideas...what the hell are we doing here in the South, raising young girls to be 'fine southern belles' only for them to end up like their mothers?" Her voice rose with every word she spat out from her mouth. She continued, "Mean-spirited, angry, hateful old biddies who beat their children to a bloody pulp because they have a different way of thinking?!" She turned to her father. "Did you know that, Daddy? Did you know that your precious southern belle has been beating your daughter like a slave, ever since she was eight?" Then she turned her hateful glare toward her mother. "You remember that, Mom? The last time you beat me because I was helping some Negroes at the country club?"

"You needed to know your place!"

"Oh, and in order to show me, you decided to beat me 'til I fell unconscious?"

"You're over-exaggerating, Chloe. It wasn't that bad—."

"For who, Mother? It wasn't that bad for who?! You selfish sack of shit!"

Her mother leaped from her rocker and headed toward Chloe with her hand raised, ready to strike.

"You hit me and I swear to God I'll be the last person you'll ever hit." Chloe's voice went low and precarious. She stood toe to toe with her mother. "Go ahead. Strike...."

They stared at each other. "I'm leaving this Godforsaken town and this Godforsaken house. I hate you most of all." And with that, Chloe slowly walked into the house. The creak of the screen door was heard opening, and then slamming shut.

Roseanne followed her sister up the stairs and to Chloe's room. Chloe pushed the door back, knowing her sister was behind her, and sat on the edge of her bed.

"What do you want?"

"Why are you acting like this?

"What way? Telling the truth?"

"You're really hurting Mom."

"Well, she forfeited the right for me to care a long time ago."

"That's not fair, Chloe."

"Hell no, it's not fair! It's not fair that my own mother hates my guts!

"She doesn't hate you. Why do you have to make things so difficult around here?"

"Please, because I have my own mind? Aren't you tired? Aren't you tired of being the perfect southern belle? Aren't *you tired, yet*?!" Chloe screamed at the top of her lungs.

Roseanne looked at her as if she didn't know this person in front of her, the one whom she shared a room with for most of her life, the one who used to sneak into her bed after their mother forbade her to, the one whom she used to protect from the other kids when they'd call her weird, the one who hid the rope and the leather switch when Mother was at it again, the one she loved and admired.

"I…I'm sorry Chloe…" She slowly turned and walked out of the room.

"Me too." Chloe sat on the edge of her bed and cried.

6

Ray and Loretta met at a dance in a small town in Louisiana. Ray was eighteen and Loretta was sixteen. She said that when she first met Ray, she didn't like him very much, but he eventually grew on her. His energy was too over the top for her. Loretta had grown up in a conservative household. Her father was a professor and her mother a housewife. She grew up in what they called a "well-to-do" environment, with lawyers and doctors and entrepreneurs. These Negro people were no slouches. They worked hard in the fall and winter, and summered at Martha's Vineyard, enjoying the fruits of their labor. Ray's family, on the other hand, were hard-nosed people who didn't take one dime for granted. He labored with his dad in running the store. His dad taught him carpentry and how to survive. Ray's mother did domestic work and, when she had time, would work alongside her husband at the store. Ray and Loretta were antithetical to each other from the start, which later caused them to question, *Was love really enough*?

"Ain't never seen you 'round here before. I'm Ray Jackson. What's your name?"

"Loretta...Loretta Forbes."

The place was jumping—sweaty Black bodies everywhere, sliding to the juke music that the band played.

"Well, Loretta, Loretta Forbes, you look like you ain't from around these parts."

"I'm here with my girlfriends."

"Hmmm, where are they?"

Pointing them out, "There...and...well, where did Junie go? I have no idea where she went to."

"It looks like they busy havin' a good time. And how 'bout you? You havin' fun?"

"Ain't quite my cup of tea."

"Oh, you used to them uppity parties where everybody drinkin' tea and eating crumpets." He laughed out loud. She joined him with a light chuckle.

"Damn, you're beautiful. Your skin is so brown, like caramel."

"Uh..."

"I'm sorry. Sometimes I just say what I'm thinkin' and..."
"No, it's all right. Thank you."

"You're quite welcome." After a slight pause, "You wanna dance?"

"I...uh..."

"Oh come on. Don't tell me you plan on puttin' a dent in this wall all night. Come on, let's cut a rug."

He took out of her hand the drink she'd been nursing all night, and pulled her onto the dance floor. They danced all night and afterward took a walk down by the lake.

"Really, where you from?"

"We live across town. My dad's a professor of philosophy and medicine at the university where we live. I'm a junior there."

"Wow! Educated and beautiful."
"You're so full of it."

He stopped her. "No, I'm not...when I first saw you, I couldn't keep my eyes off of you. You're a woman of quality, and that's rare. I know I ain't the kinda Joe you'd hang out with or anything, but if you just give me a few moments of your time..."

"I don't know...my father..."

"Wouldn't approve of a guy like me, right? A self-educated man with only an eighth grade education? Yeah, I know all too well."

She slowly looked up at him, taking him in. "You're so tall. And no, my father wouldn't approve of you. But it's my life, right?" She smiled.

"Indeed it is." A big grin rested across his face, showing even rows of pearly whites. "Indeed it is."

They kissed under that full moon that made everyone sweat and cling to one another.

They managed to secretly date for six months. They made sure to meet at a location where they knew her parents wouldn't see them together. They fell hard for one another. One day, Ray decided to surprise her at the school and waited around by the oak tree. He knew it was risky, but he had to see her. When she spotted him, she immediately ran over to him.

"What are you doing here? Are you crazy? What if my father sees you?"

"Hey, I could very well be a student you're talking to."

"Are you kidding? My father knows every face on this campus, and he'd find you quite suspicious."

"Yeah, you done for the day?"

"Yes. What do you have in mind?"

"Hmmm....come on here, gal, 'fore you get in trouble."

Ray took her to a spot along the river. He laid out a blanket, and they ate crawfish, drank beer, and talked all afternoon.

"I wanna marry you."

"Ray, we hardly know each other, and..."

"And what? You love me?"

"Why, yes, but..."

"Come on, baby, no buts. I know you're the one for me, and I don't need all year to prove otherwise. Marry me.?"

"Oh, Ray...I..."

"Two years ago before my mother passed, she told me that when I found someone special, that I make her my wife, and then she gave me this ring. Gosh, Loretta, I know I don't have much now, but I'm workin' on it. My daddy's got a store in Mississippi, and he's up in age and wants to turn it over to me. I wanna take care of you and give you things."

"Ray, it's beautiful." Gingerly, he took her by the hand and slid the ring on her finger.

"There, it fits. I knew it'd fit."

"Ray, what about my parents? They don't even know we're seeing each other."

"I'll meet him tomorrow evening."

"Ray--."

"Please, Loretta. I love you so much. I can't imagine lovin' any woman more. I've never felt this way before. I know you're the one I can spend the rest of my life with."

"Okay. But let me talk to him first. He can be real stubborn."

"Then you'll marry me?"

"Yes, Ray. I will."

"Whoowee! She said, 'yes'!!"

7

They drove up the winding road. Loretta was nervous. She couldn't believe that she'd agreed to this meeting. Ray could see that she was, so he reached for her hand while the other stayed on the steering wheel, keeping the car steady on the road.

"You all right, baby?"

"Maybe we should do it another time. Maybe we're movin' kinda fast, Ray...Maybe we should..."

"Aww, come on now, Retta. Don't do this. I knew you was gonna try to bail as soon as we got close. Don't do this baby. I love you."

Ray tried to keep the car steady, at the same time stealing glimpses at her. Finally, he slowed the car down and drove off road and parked by a beautiful willow tree. He put the car into park and turned his body around to meet hers. Loretta was still looking down, her light blue laced glove on one hand, while she wrung and twisted the other.

"Baby, please. Don't be nervous. I love you. Don't be nerv—."

"Ray," she finally turned to him. "How are we gonna do this?"

"What do you mean?"

"How are you gonna take care of me... of us?"

"I told you baby we'll be all right."

"Ray, when my father finds out what I'm up to, he'll cut me off for sure."

"Come on, Retta, it's gonna be fine. Once he sees my love for you—"

"How you gonna afford me and a baby too?"

Ray stopped. He looked at her, long and hard, "You pregnant?"

"Yes."

"Whoowee! Hot damn!"

Ray hopped out the car, waving his pageboy in the air, clicking his heels. He ran around to the other side of the car, where Loretta was, and pulled her out of the car.

"Ray, you crazy?"

"Yes…yes…"

He hoisted her off the ground, with both her feet in the air as if he were carrying her over the threshold like a new bride. He twirled her and twirled her until he lost his balance and they both tumbled on top of the tall green blades. Loretta couldn't help but laugh as she lay on her back. Ray did the same. They both laughed, while looking up at the sky. Ray stopped laughing and lay on his side, looking his beautiful bride-to-be in the face.

"I will take care of you and our baby. You gotta believe that."

"I do."

He held her close and kissed her. She invited his kiss. They stayed like that, while the breeze danced around the willow leaves.

8

Tiger decided to cut through the wooded path on his way from Mrs. Robinson's. He knew this was dangerous, but he didn't feel like going the long way home. His steps were rapid and steady. He knew his fate going through these woods and feared the worse. Steadily he moved, but then he heard a sound from behind. He stopped and looked around but saw nothing. Dusk was falling into a sullen night. He moved more rapidly and heard the rustling sound again, this time louder. He then heard a melancholic moan. "He-hello, is anybody there?" There was dead silence.

Tiger knew the game and had to move faster. With the quickness, he tried to beat the darkness, making a self-declaration to take the long way home next time. He heard the sound again and this time realized he was walking toward it and not away from it. "Hello?" He ventured again. The sound was behind the tree. He managed his nerves to see who or what it was, deterring him from his mission. Slowly, he crept behind the tree—peeking head first, then body. It was a person, all right. It was her. His heart raced. This time it was not from fear, but of desire. "How could it be?" he said to himself. "Uhh... hello?"

Maybelle looked up from her hands and saw that it was the boy who had gotten her so flagrantly reprimanded by her aunt earlier. "It's you. What are you doing here?" she said offensively.

"I take this way sometimes. Are you all right? This isn't a great place to relax and besides, it's kinda late, shouldn't you be...?"

"Please, I'm fine." She looked up at him. He saw her slightly swollen lip.

"What happened to you?"

"I told you I'm fine. Just leave me alone."

"Okay, okay. Well, I hope whatever's ailing you will turn out all right." He did an about-face to continue his short journey home.

"Hey," she yelled out.

"Yeah?" He turned around.

"I sure could use some company right now."

"Okay." Tiger sat down beside her. "You know, it's getting late. Shouldn't you be home or something? Won't your aunt and uncle be worried?"

"To hell with them, right?"

"I don't know?"

"Well, what about you? What are you doing out? Won't your folks be worried?"

"Well, they know where I'm coming from."

"And where are you coming from?" She leaned into him, laying her legs to one side and pulling them closer towards her thigh. Tiger leaned in a bit as well, allowing his body to rest beside hers.

"There's a lady named Mrs. Robinson and..."

"Oh, that lady? She gives me the creeps. My uncle told me the story of how her husband left her because she turned ugly."

"She ain't so bad."

"So what do you do for her?"

"I do stuff for her."

"Stuff? Like what kind of stuff?"

"You know. Take her groceries. My mom cooks for her and…I don't wanna talk about her."

"Okay, we don't have to. But I think it's sweet."

"Yeah." Tiger blushed a bit.

"I didn't mean to embarrass you. You sure are cute." She placed her hand over his.

"I…"

"Yes?"

"I think you're beautiful."

"I think you're great. Have you ever been with a white girl before?"

"No! I mean, it's different here. I shouldn't be here. I gotta go." He made the gesture to rise, but she gently grabbed his arm. "Please, you ain't from here and…I can't risk it, no matter how beautiful…."

"What's your name?"

"Tiger."

"Wow, is that your real name?"

"Yes. My dad named me. He said that I nearly died of some disease, shortly after I was born. Said I fought like a..."

"Tiger." She finished his sentence.

"Yes. You're not like any white girl I ever met. You're easy..."

"Easy...?"

"To talk to..."

"Of course...so are you. Your skin is beautiful and rich." She touched his cheek.

"You're..." He rubbed her hair. "I gotta go."

"I want to see you again."

"Okay, but we gotta sneak and do it."

"I'm well aware. But how?"

"Let's meet tomorrow around noon. I gotta help my father at the store, but I can meet you afterward. We can meet here and then..."

"Okay." She quickly agreed. "Until then?"

"Until then." He stood up and held out his hand. She grabbed hold of it and, with a light hoist, was pulled to her feet. They stood face to face. She kissed his cheek, turned, and skipped out of the other end of the woods.

"Until then," he said to himself.

>>>

Ray was nervous and intimidated. He knew Loretta was well-off, but he did not expect the big house or the nice neighborhood. When the two of them drove up the winding road to her home, his knees began to shake. He didn't realize it until he got out of the car and stood up, almost wobbling his six-foot-four frame to his knees. "Come on, Ray, get a grip," he said to himself. He ran around to the other side of the car and opened the door. Before he could grab her hand real good to help her out, her mother was at the door to greet them.

"Hello."

"Hi, mom. This is Ray. Ray this is—"

"Mrs. Forbes." Loretta's mother interrupted her, as if she wanted Ray to know his limits.

"Yes, ma'am. Well, it's nice to meet you, Mrs. Forbes." Ray grabbed his pageboy off his head with his left hand and extended his right hand to her. Mrs. Forbes looked at his hand and with a fin-like gesture, made the attempt to meet his hand by only touching the tip of his fingers.

"Yes, I'm sure."

"Well, I can see where Retta...uh, Loretta here gets her beauty."

"Yes, of course. Thank you."

"Mother." Loretta looked at her mother as if to tell her to play nice. "Where's Daddy?"

"He's in the study. He's expecting you." She looked at Ray, directing the statement to him. She sauntered in front of them, and when she reached the door to the study, she slowly turned the knob. "Dear, your daughter and her friend are here."

Mr. Forbes looked up from his book and slowly took the pipe out of his mouth with his right hand. His gray eyes pierced through his wife. Loretta squeezed through her mother and went straight for her father.

"Loretta, honey." Mr. Forbes had a strong and commanding presence. He was very fair, and his hair was jet black and slicked back with gray filling along the sides. Ray was shocked because Loretta's mother was as dark as licorice, which made the amalgam of Loretta's skin the color of caramel. Loretta's father's countenance intimidated Ray even more. His diction was slow and deliberate. And when he spoke, each word from his drawl lingered in the air like an ornament. Ray felt his heart beating in his head, his hands, his stomach, and his feet. His palms were sweaty, so every now and then he wiped them on his pant leg, one by one, alternating one hand and then the other. And when it was time for him to shake Mr. Forbes's hand, he double-wiped and extended his right hand, while he clutched his hat in his left.

"Yes, sir. How do you do?"

Mr. Forbes noticed Ray's uneasiness and did not feel the need to make him feel at ease; after all, this young man was involved with his sweet Loretta, his only daughter, his only child.

"Please, have a seat." Mr. Forbes insisted. "Loretta, why don't you wait outside while Ray and I become more acquainted?

"All right, Daddy." She tiptoed to kiss him on the cheek and stared at him with one eyebrow up that read, "Don't be too hard on him." Mr. Forbes gave her a look that said, "Don't worry."

While walking out, she smiled at Ray, which briefly put him at ease until he heard Mr. Forbes clear his voice.

"I really love—."

"Please, son. Don't talk. Look, Loretta is my only child and I want only the best for her."

"Yes sir, that's why—."

"How much?"

"Sir?"

"How much? Obviously you want or need money. How much will it cost you to leave my daughter alone?

"I don't understand. You're gonna pay me to keep away from your daughter?"

"It doesn't matter. Just name your price. I'll give you $5,000." Mr. Forbes took out his checkbook and grabbed a pen off his desk.

"What the hell is going on? Mr. Forbes, I don't want to leave your daughter alone. I love her. I'm here to ask you for Loretta's hand in marriage. I love her."

"I don't think that will be a good idea. You see, Loretta is refined and well-educated. I have spent years—just take the money and I will tell her that you changed your mind. You can take the money and slip out the back door. Sure she'll be sad, but I'm certain she'll get over it."

"Are we seriously having this conversation? I..."

"Why are you here? This is absolutely ridiculous. What are you, some kind of a fling?"

"Sir, Loretta and I are serious. We…"

"How can you be serious when Loretta is engaged to be married to Toby Wallace?"

"What?!"

"Yes. I didn't want to hurt your feelings. Listen son, you're not the first person she's dragged into a mess. She is infamous for doing things like this. I just didn't think that she'd sink… Well, you understand. I tell you what. I will still give you the money for your trouble and…"

"I don't believe you." Ray said under his breath.

"Excuse me, what?!"

"I said, I don't believe you! In fact, I don't believe anything you're sayin'. Loretta loves me and I am crazy about her."

"What you are is just crazy." He walked closer to Ray and there they stood, toe to toe.

"Look... Mr. Forbes" moving back a bit, "I love Loretta and I'm gonna do right by her."

"What the hell are you talking about? She doesn't need the likes of you to do anything for her. She's got me, her father."

"Mr. Forbes, she's pregnant.

"Who's pregnant?!"

"Loretta..."

"You sonofabitch! You take that back. Loretta wouldn't do that to me. You sonofabitch!

"You don't understand. I love her and I'm gonna do right--."

Mr. Forbes swung at Ray and missed. He swung again, and Ray pushed him into the desk. Mr. Forbes charged at him. They both tumbled on to the floor and rolled toward the floor-to-ceiling bookcase. Loretta and her mother ran into the room to see what the commotion was. They found both men scrambling on top of one another. Mr. Forbes had Ray by the neck, while Ray tried to fight him off.

"Oh my God, Daddy! Let him go! Let him go!"

"Benjamin, what are you doing?! Let him go!"

"Hell no, he's a liar! A liar!"

"What are you talking about, Benjamin?" Let him go!" His wife ran to the grappling pair and pried her husband's hands from around Ray's neck. "Do you want to go to jail?"

"I'm gonna kill him! I'm gonna kill him..." He allowed her hands to pry his from around Ray's neck. Mr. Forbes, feeling destitute, no longer in control, rolled to one side and sobbed uncontrollably. Ray leaned against the bookcase, gasping for air. Loretta held him in her arms, trying to help his breathing.

"Is it true?" Mr. Forbes asked in a dejected tone. His head was still down as the tears fell from his face. His heart was broken, and he couldn't contain himself. He was a man of prestige, of stature. He was well respected in his community, a master of science and medicine as well as philosophy. His father, a medical doctor, was a white man, who was shunned by his father for marrying a black woman. Now, Mr. Forbes wanted the best for his family. He wanted his daughter to marry wealthy. He'd handpicked Toby Wallace to be her husband.

Loretta hated Toby. He was short and stout. Not only that, he talked with an annoying lisp. Whenever they walked together, she would hang her head down in embarrassment. Toby was extremely arrogant as well as highly intelligent and was studying to be a doctor.

Mr. Forbes had arranged it. It was settled. He had no idea that his daughter had other plans. The daughter he had bounced on his knee when she could hardly walk. The daughter he had crooned to sleep every night. The side that no one, not even his wife, had ever seen. The daughter whom he took long walks with, told jokes to. In fact, he was closer to her than to his own wife. Mrs. Forbes hated their relationship, but she could never bring herself to say anything. It was too painful.

"Is what true, Benjamin? Why are you harassing this young man?"

"Because, Angela, he claims to have gotten Loretta pr...pre....pregnant."

"Loretta, what is your father talking about?"

"Mom, I...I am."

"Oh, Loretta..."

"Mom, I love him. It just happened. I want this. I want Ray."

"Get out!"

"Benjamin, please..."

"Shut up... you shut up! You, get out!!"

"That is your daughter. You can't talk to her like that!"

"I can talk to that little bitch any way I want. She is not my daughter! *She is not my daughter*!"

"Daddy please." She rushed over to him and knelt beside him. "Daddy, I'm still me. I'm still Loretta. You can't say that to me."

"How could you? How could you do this?" He buried his face in her stomach and cried. She looked at him and, with brief hesitation, rubbed his hair with her left hand while bracing herself with her right. Mrs. Forbes and Ray watched as the two displayed an affection that was incomprehensible to both of them. Her father held her tighter. He lost himself and moved his hand between her legs and gripped her crotch. *"You fucking whore!"* He squeezed tighter, and Loretta screamed, trying to squirm away from the leviathan grip he had between her legs.

"Benjamin, what are you doing?" his wife cried.

"Nobody can have her," he screamed.

Ray ran over to Mr. Forbes and pulled him off her. He slammed him on his back, while beating his head against the floor. Mr. Forbes surrendered to the attack and fell semi-unconscious. Mrs. Forbes ran over to Ray and pulled him off her husband. Cries and moans rang around the study. Ray stood up and walked over to Loretta.

He held out his hand. She studied it and then put her hand in his. Gently, he pulled her up from the floor. She leaned on him as they walked towards the double doors that led out of the study.

"Ma'am," he said to Mrs. Forbes as they both walked past her, to the foyer, and out the front door. Loretta never looked back.

9

I woke up early, making sure that all of my chores were done before meeting Maybelle. Why was I still going through with this, knowing the consequences? But the more I wrestled with those thoughts, the more excited I got. I wanted to meet her, but what if it was a trick? I've known Negro boys who was trapped into meeting white girls and their bodies were found at the bottom of a river or hangin' from a tree. But she was different. She didn't seem like the type to lure anybody into nothin'. She seemed genuine and awful beautiful. I felt good when I was with her. I figured that maybe her aunt and uncle might give me a chance once they got to know me and...hell, I knew them, and they was just about as racist as...

"Tiger?"

"Momma, I'm gettin' dressed. He covered his chest with his shirt.

"Boy, ain't nothin' you got I ain't seen before. What you doing up so early?"

Loretta noticed his attire. "Why are you getting dressed in your good shirt?"

"Nothing," he said, not looking directly at her.

"Don't you 'nothing' me, boy. I know you ain't gonna meet your father like that to work in the store today…"

"No. I mean. I'm gonna meet dad. But I'm gonna meet some friends after. Is that all right?"

"And when were you gonna let me in on this, Tiger?"

"Well, I'm tellin' you now. Can I meet some friends when I'm done helpin' Dad?"

"I don't care, but don't stay out too late."

Tiger's mind was preoccupied and did not hear his mother's answer.

"You hear me, Tiger?"

"Huh… yeah, sure, Momma."

"What has gotten into you?"

"I'm fine. I just got a lot to do before I meet up with the guys. You think Dad would mind if I left early? I wanted to meet up with my friends around noon."

"What is with you all of a sudden? What is it that you have to agitate what was already planned? Your father hardly sees you as it is."

"And whose fault is that?"

His mother glared at him. Her eyes began to well.

"Momma, I didn't mean it. I..."

"No, you're right. It's not your fault or the girls'. It's no one's fault but me and your father's."

"Don't you miss him, Momma?"

"Like crazy. You know, we were married for eight days when we had our first fight. He wanted to hang out with his friends, and I wanted him to stay in and... well, we got into this big fight, and he stormed out of the house. When he came home, he told me that we should never allow a fight to tear us apart. So we vowed to always talk things out, and when we couldn't, we'd leave it until later, but never the next day."

"It's been almost a week. What made you guys break your promise to one another?" Tiger sat on the edge of his bed, putting on his shoes.

"Your father is just being silly. He's too insecure."

"About what?"

"I don't want to talk about this, Tiger."

"Gee, you sound like Dad. What's the matter with you people?!" Tiger knew he shouldn't talk that way, but he was frustrated and needed his family under one roof.

"It's not fair, I know. But..."

"Whatever. You two are the experts. I'm done with it." He left his mother standing in the middle of his room.

>>>

Tiger started up the road to meet his father at the store but decided against it. Those two made him angry, and he didn't want to see neither one of them at the moment. So, he ventured a left to where he'd hoped Maybelle would be, standing at the doorway of her uncle's store. He took a huge chance, and his hunch was correct—

she was on the top step, in a light blue dress, barefoot and free. Tiger stood at a distance and watched her while she teased and ran her fingers through her hair, leaning her head back, allowing the sun to bathe her creamy white skin. He made sure that no one was around, and then he came closer.

"Let's get outta here."

She opened her eyes, "Tiger, what are you doing...?"

"Come on, let's go." He held out his dark hand. A smile came across her red lips. She grabbed her shoes and quickly put them on her feet. They both ran down the road toward the lake.

10

Chloe hadn't seen her family in a year and was excited and nervous about going back to Mississippi. She wasn't around to walk across the stage for graduation, so her diploma was sent by way of Roseanne. When Roseanne presented the diploma to her parents, Father grunted and Mother folded her arms. "Burn it. She didn't care about stayin' around to get it. It ain't no good now." Roseanne, of course, kept it until Chloe decided to come to her senses and returned home from her rebellious excursion. With bitter anger, Roseanne tucked the diploma in her third bureau drawer, along with the keepsakes that William had given her over the two-years' time of their courtship.

And now, Chloe had decided to come home—and with a surprise! Roseanne was the one who received the letter and read it out loud to her parents. Father was pleasantly pleased. Mother, however, began cursing the prodigal daughter and replied,

"What the hell she done got herself into this time?" She continued, "Knowing her, she probably done decided to do somethin' outlandish like...joinin' a convent or somethin'." Even with her mother's bitterness, Roseanne wasn't discouraged. She continued to read on, and then the letter stopped, abruptly—as if Chloe were listening to her mother's disapproving comments. Roseanne looked in the envelope for the rest, but there wasn't a continuation. *So many unanswered questions,* she thought.

"What happened?" Roseanne asked. "Why did she stop the letter?"

"Maybe she just got caught up with somethin'," Father interjected.

"She was always insensitive," added Mother. "Well, she can stay where she is for all I care."

"Why do you say such things?" Roseanne said, hurt.

"What do you mean?"

"You know what I mean."

"No. Why don't you explain yourself, Missy, since you got so much to say?"

"You two don't start," Father chimed in, trying to keep the peace of what was left of the family.

"No, I want to hear what she has to say. I want to hear her tell me how to be a better mother." Roseanne felt a twinge of intimidation disagreeing with her mother; however, for Chloe's sake, felt that she needed to stand up to her once and for all.

"I don't like it when you all fuss the way that you do. We are family," Father interrupted, trying to smooth any potential escalation.

"Family?" Roseanne exploded. "You wouldn't think so what with the way she talks, as if her child is a complete stranger."

"How can you talk that way? Father and I have always given you everything you wanted," Mother said with hurt in her voice.

"I'm not your only daughter, Mother." Roseanne stormed into the house.

"She's right," Father said. "What's wrong with you? Why do you hate Chloe so much?"

Mother sat down and began to ponder the words spoken to her by her first love. "I...I don't hate her, Father. She's my baby. I was happy with her in me. I just don't know. Somewhere down the line she disappointed me with her behavior. She's different, and I guess I don't understand her ways. She doesn't have those values that I tried to instill. I mean, her sister got it. Why couldn't..." Suddenly she paused. "You want fried chicken this evenin'"?

"I want to know what you're thinkin' still," Father gently said.

"Apples look good at the market, and I was thinkin' of bakin' a pie." She continued ignoring him.

"Damn it, Mother, I want you to finish!" Father screamed at his cold and disheartened wife of twenty-three years. "I can't believe that you can just dismiss all that was said to fried chicken and apple pie. I can starve if it means you telling me what's on your mind after all this time."

With that, Mother rose out of her present position and casually walked from the porch and into her haven—herself.

>>>

"She's here! She's here!" squealed Roseanne as Chloe drove up in a top model Ford.

Father ran from the study. He had come home extra early from the mill, making sure he didn't miss a thing. "There's my girl." Father said with a grin so wide that Roseanne thought he would break a jawbone. "Here she comes, Rosie." Father said with excitement. Roseanne looked at her father with a bit of jealousy and, for a brief moment, wished that she were in her sister's shoes, just to see her father look at her in that way. But that was just what it was—brief. Her sister had come home and with a surprise. She wondered what it was. As Chloe made her way up the road in her car, William wasn't far behind. *This was so perfect*, thought Roseanne, *All the people that I care about the most are going to be in one room this evening.* Chloe scurried out the car and gave her little sister a great big southern hug. They both squeezed each other tightly, while jumping around, almost plummeting to the ground. Chloe grabbed onto the wooden railing attached to the porch.

"Girl, you almost made us fall for dear life. Where'd you get off having strength like that?"

"I don't know? Just happy to see you is all."

"It's all right. I'd rather a greeting like that any day of the week." As the words rang through the air, Chloe's surprise came waltzing behind her.

"I thought that you both were going to tumble to the ground."

Everyone froze.

"Oh, this is Julian Wright...my husband." All jaws dropped. "I know I didn't explain in the letter. I just wanted to show you rather than tell you in some silly old letter, you know?" To Roseanne, "See, now we'll both be married women. When are you and William tying the nuptials?"

What was she talking about? Roseanne thought. *"Tying the nuptials...silly old letter?" That letter meant a lot to me.* "It was hardly silly."

"What's that, Roseanne?" Chloe asked.

"I said, it was hardly silly."

"What?"

"The letter. It was hardly silly."

"Oh, Roseanne, you're still so sentimental."

"And who is this?" William broke through the awkwardness to shake Julian's hand.

"Good to make your acquaintance." Julian began to look around. "Wow, this is something out of a Rockwell painting. I mean the house and the trees and all." Everyone but Chloe looked at him strangely. But he didn't notice a thing. "And look, is that a weeping willow tree? Being from the city, I don't get to see many of those...well, none of this for that matter." He laughed.

"Why, yes it is," Father broke out of his trance brought on by his daughter being married. "It's seventy years old. Come on inside so we can get better acquainted."

"I can't wait!" Julian said enthusiastically. "It's been a while since I've had a home-cooked meal."

"Why, Julian, you'll make my family think I'm starvin' you half to death."

"Aww, baby. You're swell and all, but you do need a little help in the kitchen department."

"Hmm, well I don't think you married me for my cookin'" They both laughed. Julian forgot himself and kissed her on the neck, while he felt her behind. "Stop, baby." They both looked up to the family watching with embarrassment.

"Well you're in for a treat." Father broke the awkwardness. "Her mother is the best cook this side of Mississippi."

Everyone else led the way, while the newlyweds trailed behind. It was as if they wanted to either hide or surprise Mother with the shocking, yet bewildering news of Chloe's newly sprung marriage.

11

Their run turned to a slow pace. Maybelle slipped her arm underneath Tiger's, while his hands stayed in his pockets. The silence between them spoke louder than what was going through both their heads. They reached the bottom of the hill and sat at the edge of the lake. The sun blazed; however, there was a slight breeze that rippled the water. Tiger picked up a stick and tossed it in the water. More ripples formed. Maybelle placed her head on his shoulder, and then she began.

"Are you okay?"

"Sure."

"You're nervous."

"Yes."

The silence began again.

"It's so beautiful out here. There's nothing like this in New Jersey. I mean, we have stuff, but not like this. You must love growing up here."

"It's unfair out here, being Colored."

"What do you mean?"

"You know what lynching is?"
 "What?"
"Lynching, do you know what it is?"
"Well, I..."
"It's when a man, preferably a Colored, is hung from a tree. Something as beautiful as the one we're sitting under right now. Sometimes, he is thrown at the bottom of a lake, much like the one you're admiring right now. Or dragged from a car, or burned to a tree..."
"That's awful."
"It's inhumane."
"My mother told me stories. About how she had to leave because of a tragic incident that happened when she was younger. She said the South can be so cruel. She calls it the 'dirty South.'"
"Perfect name for it. What does your dad think?"
"I don't know. He died before I was born."
"Wow, I'm sorry."
"It's okay."
 "Do you know anything about him?"

"Uh...not really."

"Aren't you curious?"

"I don't know. I guess. Maybe?"

"I would be."

"Yeah." Maybelle became silent.

Tiger leaned against the seventy-five-year-old tree, uprooting the blades of grass. He opened the palm of his hand and let the grass fall between his fingers.

"What are we doing?"

"We're sitting here, getting to know one another."

"You know this can never work, right?"

"I've known worse to happen."

"Nothing worse than this. If we're caught, we could do a lot of damage in this town. What's more, I could be killed."

"I'm only here for the summer. Maybe you can come back with me."

"I live here. My family is here." He turned to her. "I want to do things, Maybelle. I want to be a writer, or a teacher, or a professor at a college. This is crazy. I do like you, but this is crazy. What if something happens before you leave? What if...?"

"Nothing will happen because we won't let it. We'll be careful." She turned to him and rubbed the side of his cheek. He looked at her and pulled her closer to him. And like the pull of gravity or a magnet to steel, so did their lips meet. There, along the perfect spot—amidst the tall grass and the wildflowers, beneath the azure sky; right underneath the weeping willow that swayed back and forth to the rhythm of the breeze. Theirs was a kiss that could inspire the hopeless romantic or repulse the traditional hater. Whatever the case, it was a secret shared only with nature.

>>>

"I am so impressed with this meal," Julian exclaimed as he stuffed his face with a soft buttered biscuit that Mother had made from scratch, along with everything else on the table.

"Thank you...Julian, is it? Mother responded.

"Yes, ma'am."

"What an unusual name."

"My father named me."

"Interesting. And please, have more potatoes," she offered in her most congenial way.

"Oh God, no, Mrs. Clemens. I couldn't eat another bite," he said while he leaned back in his chair.

"Yes, my mother does well in the kitchen." Chloe said proudly. She was more proud that her mother was on her best southern behavior. She had always known that even if her mother was ticked at something, she could somehow pull it together in front of company, which was the one trait of her mother's that wasn't inherent in her.

"Well, this is a really fine home you've made for your family, Mr. Clemens!" Julian exclaimed.

"Why, thank you. I suppose you've done the same for my little girl, beings I see that smile on her face and all." Father reached over and touched Chloe's hand. "I reckon this marriage done did her good." Chloe smiled.

"So," Mother chimed in, "what do you do for a living?"

"I'm an investment banker," he said vigorously.

"Julian graduated from Yale—the top of his class," Chloe added.

"Oh sweetheart, nobody wants to hear that."

"Well, that's impressive," William said. "I did all right in school, but I never went to no Yale or nothin' like that. So, you think that you can give me some tips on managing my money, since I'll be takin' on a family real soon and all?" He held Roseanne real close to him.

"William, please."

"Ah, come on honey. You know how it is. A man's gotta protect his investment!"

Roseanne became agitated by the whole evening. She couldn't understand why everyone was being so accepting of this union and not asking questions.

"So Sis, when was the big day? I mean, how did you two meet? It just all seems so sudden. Don't you think the whole thing seems sudden, Mother?" Roseanne turned to her mother, hoping for her to help with the ambush that she was creating on Chloe.

"Which would you like for me to answer first, Roseanne?" Chloe said, a bit agitated.

"Oh, it doesn't matter to me—to us for that matter." Roseanne sat back in her chair and began to look around, but to her dismay, no one seemed to share her enthusiasm to get to the meat of Chloe's new life.

Roseanne rose up from the table. "I can't believe you people. I can't believe that after a whole year, no one cares that she's shown up with this...this...man?"

"Excuse me, Roseanne!" Chloe retorted. "But this is my husband, and I think you're being rude."

"Come on, Rosie," William said, trying to calm her down.

"No, you don't tell me to calm down. You weren't here when Daddy was sick with worry because his baby girl decided to walk out to chase some two-bit dream of becoming a poet. Tell me, Sis, publish anything lately, or were you too busy trying to catch yourself a really big, rich fish?" Chloe stared at her sister and got up from the table and walked around to her side.

"What?!"

Roseanne got up to meet her sister. They were face to face. Chloe raised her hand and slapped Roseanne across the face. Roseanne held her face, shocked at her sister's action. The room was still. "How dare you judge me," Chloe cried. "Now you have a strong mind after all of these brainwashed years of doing the 'right thing,' you...hypocrite?!"

"Stop it, the both of you!" Father cried. "This is supposed to be a happy occasion, and you two are fighting like a bunch of wild hogs." Everyone grew still. "Rosie's right," he found his voice again. "I have been sick with worry, but that doesn't give you the right to express my feelings in front of company," he said to Roseanne. "I just thank God that you're safe, happy, and..."

Chloe ran from the table and into the bathroom across the hall. Everyone was stunned. After a while, she finally returned to the dinner table. Her husband stood to help her to be seated. He rubbed her back, while she placed her head on his shoulder. He looked at her inquisitively and with a twinge of tension.

"Honey, are you okay?"

"I'll be fine."

"Here, drink some water."

"I don't know who y'all think you're foolin'. That girl is pregnant," Mother said with disdain.

"Pregnant?" Roseanne said shocked.

Chloe put her head down as if she was ashamed. "Yes, I am." She looked at her husband. His inquisitive and palpable stare sent a chill through her.

"You didn't tell me?"

"No, I wanted to..."

"Please don't say, surprise me." He said in a low and slow tone. "I don't like those."

"You don't seem too pleased?" Mother broke their side discussion.

"I...well...yes. Of course I am. We've been waiting...I or we, rather, weren't expecting so soon."

"Just messes up your perfect little life?" Mother antagonized. "I mean, ain't that what you do when you get married, you have children, right? What's the wait for? You certainly didn't wait to get married!"

"Oh, here we go! I knew you couldn't hold your true colors."

"You don't tell me about what's true. You waltz in here with your fake life and your fake husband and now you're pregnant and it ain't the right timing?"

"Don't start, Mother! I'm getting outta here."

"No, Chloe," Father said, then turned to his wife. "Damn it, Mother! Why are you like this? Why do you say such things?"

Mother continued eating the dinner she'd prepared, unashamed of her actions. "Why the hell are you all looking around for? Ain't nothin' been said wrong here. Chloe has done a dishonorable thing by coming here and flaunting that man and her unborn child 'round here." To Julian, "Tell me, dear, are you sure it's yours?"

"Mrs. Clemens, I won't have you talk to my wife like this. From what I can see, the best thing that has come out of you is Chloe—it's certainly not your manners." He turned to his wife, who was now looking pale and despondent. "Let's go, baby." He helped her to her feet. She leaned her head on his shoulder, while the two of them made their way toward the front door. Everyone was in a frozen state, except for Mother, who continued eating her dinner. Chloe looked back once more before opening the door. She felt a slight twinge in the pit of her stomach and then opened the door. The sun felt good against her skin. Julian eased her down the stairs and into the backseat so she could lie down. He quickly moved around to the driver's side and peeled off. Roseanne ran to the door and watched them drive away. Once again, she was without her sister.

12

Tiger sat under the green, mossy willow tree, its leaves tickling the grass below. Maybelle rested her head on his thigh, holding his hand on top of her chest. It was a relaxed setting as he tried reciting a poem by Robert Frost.

Two roads diverged in a yellow wood,
And sorry I could not travel both
And be one traveler, long I stood
And looked down as far as I could

To where it bent in the undergrowth...
"I can't remember the rest..." He began to rub her golden locks, while she continued rubbing his arm.

"That was great anyway. I love that poem."

"Yeah, I had to memorize it in the ninth grade. I guess I forgot it."

"It's okay. It's kinda speakin' about us, huh?"

"What do you mean?"

"I mean the poem, making decisions and everything."

"Yeah..."

Maybelle hoisted her head from Tiger's lap to look at him dead on. "You don't have to be afraid. I won't let anything happen to you. I mean, I know we've only known each other a few days, but...I'm falling for you real fast and...I just never felt like this before."

"Me neither. Maybe it's just new and different."

"Maybe. But whatever the case, I know I want to feel like this forever."

"It's too risky, Maybelle. I want to do things, great things. But I can't do them if..." He looked up at the tree he was sitting under.

"Tiger, don't say that. Maybelle said in a whisper. "Why do you say such things? Why do you need to be so drastic?"

"I'm not."

"Oh, here we go again. Why do we have to talk like this every time we get together? Why can't we just be...?"

"Normal? Because it ain't normal, Maybelle. Obviously you don't get it! You can do whatever you want because you're white. You don't have to deal with whites calling you a 'nigger' or 'boy,' no matter your age or status. What do you have to ever worry about, Maybelle? You live in New Jersey and you're white!"

"Well, I'm not going to apologize for who I am, Tiger. I can't help that."

"And I'm not asking you to. All I'm asking is that you try to understand."

She looked at him inquisitively. She tried to understand, but she couldn't wrap her brain around the ways of the South.

"Somebody gotta look at this thing with both eyes opened. Besides, can you honestly go home and tell your racist aunt and uncle that you're falling for a nice Colored boy? I'd be dead before the sun hits the sky."

Tears fell from Maybelle's eyes. He reached his hand to her cheek and wiped her eyes. "Please don't cry. I'm sorry."

"Don't do this," she pleaded, "because it sounds like you're breaking up with me before we've really begun."

"I'm trying to stop something that could potentially hurt us both, especially me," he continued, "and if you cared for me the way you say, then you'd let this thing go."

"I see that you can be cold when you want to be." She turned her back to him.

Tiger wanted to reach out to her but decided against it. They'd just be going in circles.

"I gotta go home. My mom's probably wondering where I am." He hoisted himself up and held out his hand to help her, but she didn't respond to it.

"So is this it?" She stayed on the ground, staring at the flowers on her favorite pale blue dress.

"I...guess." He held out his hand once more and she took it this time. He pulled her up, and they were face to face.

"Tiger please don't do this to me...to us."

"I can't jeopardize my life—and yours, for that matter. I want you to be able to experience a full and happy life. You can't do that if you're turned away by your family. I have to think this way because this is the only way. Besides, you're only here for the summer. It's just all in vain."

"It was never that. The way I feel for you is not in vain. And I'm not afraid of my bigot family. Do you believe in soul mates?"

"Yes."

"I feel that you're my soul mate."

Tiger couldn't risk it. He knew the laws of the South and that to be with a white was a necktie party for sure. While these thoughts rushed in and out of his mind and through his heart, he felt something wet roll down his cheek.

"I waited a long time to meet someone like you. Perhaps I have a different fate in this crazy world."

"Perhaps we both do." She kissed the cheek where the tear rolled down and held him tight.

13

Ray sat on the stoop of his storefront, thinking of the conversation between him and Loretta. The more his mind wandered the angrier he became. How could she want to go home after what that man did to us? He couldn't believe how unrealistic and insensitive she was being. Loretta's father was dying, and despite of all feelings in the past, she needed to see him. Mr. Forbes needed Loretta to take over his affairs after he passed away—at least, that's what the letter said, that Ray found under his wife's pillow. "That bastard," mumbled Ray. He thought about the rest of the letter and balled his fist up and smacked it in the palm of the other.

"Are you okay?"

Ray looked up to find a beautiful, tall, slender white woman with red hair, looking right at him and standing at the bottom of the stair.

"Hello." He stood up quickly.

"Hello. Somebody make you mad?"

"Oh, I'm fine. May I help you with anything?"

"Yes, I need some snacks for my trip."

"A trip, is it a long one?"

"Yes. I'm going to New York."

"Wow, New York. That's a long way from Mississippi."

"Yes. I was shooting as far as the moon, but I don't think my car can handle the ride." They both laughed.

He opened the screen door for her to enter, while following behind.

"Hey, there's a "white only" store up the road from here.

"I know. I drove right past it. Then I saw you sitting on the stair of this store and decided that you could use the company more than that guy up the road, right?"

"Well..."

"Of course you could." She smiled at him with the most beautiful smile he'd ever seen.

"Please," he let her in first, "help yourself to whatever you need."

"Thank you, sir. You're too kind." She curtsied in front of him. His head went back, and out came a hearty laugh.

She rose and looked at him. "That's nice."

"What?"

"Your laugh. It's nice." She smiled again.

"That's also nice."

"What?"

"Your smile."

"Thank you."

He looked at her and found himself looking in the wrong way. Suddenly, he broke the gaze. "So are you from here? I mean, I've never seen you around town before."

"Oh please, I'm not. I'm from Chicago, by way of Florida."

"Okay. New York, Florida, Chicago… are you some kind of a performer or something?"

"Uhn, I wish it were that simple and glamorous. Actually, I was following a guy, but it turned out to be a bust."

"I'm sorry to hear."

"Don't be. Hey, how about we celebrate with one of them pops in that cooler?" she said. "My treat!"

"Sure thing, but how's 'bout them being on me, instead?"

"Okay, whatever makes you happy?" she responded.

Ray went into the icebox and took out two pops. He opened them with the bottle opener that hung on the side of it, and handed her one. He took his rightful place behind the counter, while she found a place on one of the stools.

"Happy," he said, grinning a bit.

"What's that you say?"

"You said, 'whatever makes me happy.' I hadn't been that for a while now."

"Why?"

He looked at her, knowing that he shouldn't be doing this. But it'd been a while since someone was interested in his point of view, his thoughts...his feelings.

"My wife wants to move back to Louisiana, and..."

"And what?" Peering intently at him.

"And I just don't think it's right. I mean, I know her father is dying, but he was such a bastard when we left him. Do you know he had the nerve to…" He realized what he was doing. "Oh, I'm so sorry. I don't even know you and I'm going on and on."

"No, it's fine. Nice to hear someone else's problems for a change instead of turning mine over and over in my head."

"So say it out loud." Ray took a swig of his soda.

"Okay…well, it's simple. I was living in Chicago. Minding my business, you know? And then I saw this great-looking guy with the most amazing drawl, kinda like yours." She stared at Ray. Ray became a bit uncomfortable but didn't turn away. "Anyway, he walked into my salon to meet one of the girls he was seeing. He said, 'Howdy,' to me and that was it." She laughed embarrassingly, "Stupid, right?"

"No. And then what happened?"

"Well, I sold the salon and ran off with the jerk. Turned out, the drawl was fake and so were his feelings for me."

"Wow, I'm sorry. You sold your store?

"Yes...."

"Wow."

"Well, if my wife stays in Louisiana, I may end up having to sell this place, too. But I don't think that I could bring myself to do it."

"Do you love her?"

"With everything in me."

"Then what's the problem?"

"Here, you've got some..." He didn't finish his sentence, but grabbed a napkin out of the dispenser and leaned into her to wipe her chin. She held his hand, and looked directly into his eyes. Ray was uncomfortable.

"I'm sorry. I didn't..."

"No..." he said, "It's...I mean, It's okay..."

"You just have the kindest eyes. You couldn't hurt anyone," she said gingerly.

"Thank you."

"Your wife is lucky."

"Well, that fool is the one who missed out."

"You know, things always have a way of working themselves out. And just by talking to you I can see that you're a caring and gentle man who loves his family."

"All that doesn't matter now." His head went down.

"It always matters." She gently squeezed his hand. He didn't pull away. It felt good—her holding his hand with her long, slender white hand.

"I..."

"What?"

"I shouldn't be..."

"It's okay. Besides, we're not doing anything wrong."

"I'm married. I'm lonely and...I'm married." He took his hand away.

"I know."

"Hey, it's not you. You are very pretty and refreshing. I just don't want to push my woes on you or give you the wrong impression."

"I'm a big girl."

They continued to stare at one another. She leaned in a bit closer and just before the inevitable occurred—

"Dad, what are you doing?!"

"Tiger?" Ray said, startled. "I...it's not what you think."

"Who the hell is this? Is this the reason why you and mom...?

"Wait a minute, boy. I told you it's not what you think."

"So tell me, what am I thinking?"

"I'd better be going." She leaned into him, "Maybe I'll try the white guy up the road." She smiled. "Thank you for the pop." To Tiger. 'It's not his fault," while looking at Ray, "he was the perfect gentleman." She walked out of the store and to her car. Ray followed behind her and watched her ease into the red convertible. She took one more glance at him and waved goodbye. He waved back briefly, forgetting his son was in the store. Ray was enchanted, if only for a moment, by this mysterious woman. He continued his stare as she drove away, leaving her smoke and perfume behind.

"Dad?" Tiger broke his father's trance. "What were you doing with that woman?"

"She was just passing through. She's not from here."

"What was going on?"

"Look Tiger, nothing happened, all right?"

"Yeah, I walked in."

"Don't start with me."

"What do you mean, don't start with you? You were really close to kissing that woman, and you tell me not to start? It looked like you were starting something."

"It was totally innocent. Nothing happened." He busied himself around the store, throwing away the items that were used during the beautiful-strange visit.

"Don't walk away from me!" He grabbed his father by the arm. "You owe me an explanation. How could you do this to mom...to our family?"

"I'm not doing anything!" He pushed his son and knocked him into the shelf.

Canned goods spilled from the shelf and onto Tiger's shoulders and arms. "It's your mother." Not realizing what he did. "She's the one who's messing things up. She's the one who's making life a living hell for this family! I love her. I love this family. I worked hard to try to give you all everything!"

"Don't try to change the subject by blaming what I just saw on Mom, you sonofabitch!" Ray ran over to where Tiger stood and backhanded him so hard that Tiger plummeted to the floor. "As long as you are my son, you will talk to me civil. You understand me?"

"Fine." He cried.

Ray noticed that his cry was not from what just occurred, but from something else. He bent down and cradled his son in his arms. Tiger held on to his father for dear life—allowing him to save him from his pain.

14

Julian took Chloe out of there. He couldn't stand the ridicule any longer, and neither could she for that matter. He couldn't understand how her family could be so cruel, especially a mother. While driving down the road, he watched Chloe through the rear-view mirror with her head against the window. With remnants of teardrops glued to her face, she held his handkerchief delicately in her hand, staring far and away.

"I'm sorry about what happened. I'm sorry that I pressed you to see your folks."

Julian chose his words so as not to dismay Chloe more than she already was. His being sorry did nothing for her; instead, she rubbed her forehead and then placed her head in between her knees.

"You have a headache?" he asked with concern. "I saw a pharmacy earlier on. Why don't I stop to see what the pharmacist can recommend, beings that you're...well." He continued to steal glances at her through the rear-view mirror. "Is that all right?"

"It doesn't matter," she said with her head still between her knees.

"Well, I'll think for both of us. I'm going to make the stop and maybe by then you'll care." Julian drove fifteen minutes more into town and spotted the pharmacy. He parked the car across the street and before getting out, called to her.

"Chloe? Chloe?" Gently, he shook her.

"What happened?"

"You fell asleep with your head between your legs. Why don't you stretch out? I'll find a hotel around here so that we can stay the night and tomorrow, first thing, we'll head out. Is that all right or does it still not matter?"

She smiled at him because she loved it when he took charge, yet wanted to include her in the decision-making.

"I'm sorry, sweetheart," she said, "of course it matters, and it sounds good to me, except I want to come up front with you."

"Okay, whatever you want. I'll be back." He kissed her on the forehead and began on his quest. Looking at him taking quick strides across the street, she smiled while thinking how lucky she was to have a man like him. She was too tired to move, but rather closed her eyes and drifted off to sleep.

>>>

Twenty minutes later she opened her eyes and found that they were still parked in the same spot. She became annoyed and wondered what was taking her husband so long at the pharmacy. She focused her eyes and saw him in front of the store, talking to a woman—a Colored woman.

"Danny, what are you doing here?"

"I told you not to call me that—it's Julian, and I'm just passing through. I'm not staying."

"Passing—you can say that again."

"Don't start, Stella."

"You're not going to stay long enough to see Ma'dear?"

"I told you, I don't have time. Just tell her I came through and I'll see her in a few months or so."

"How can you do this? How can you live with yourself? Passing?"

"Look, Stella, we've been through this a hundred times. I'm only seizing an opportunity to do better for myself. Coloreds don't have the same opportunities as whites. I just so happened to have the best of the better world. It doesn't mean that I'm any less Colored than, say..."

"I am? I can't believe we're related and you're talking and acting like this. You're even looking around to see who is watching. You're pathetic."

"I don't have time to get into it with you. I promise that I'll visit next time I'm in town, and then you can wave your judgmental finger all over Mississippi. Right now, I have a lot of things on my plate, what with work at the bank and all."

"Hey, the only reason why you got that job is because you're a perpetrator and a fraud."

"Maybe you should feel lucky that someone like me got out from under. And how can you talk to me like this, after all the money I send you and Ma'dear's way? I even paid your way through medical school.

"Look *Julian*, it's not that I'm ungrateful or anything, I just want you to be true to yourself. You *are* coming to my graduation right?"

"I don't know—if work doesn't hold me."

"Don't you mean your color?"

"I gotta go. I'm doing the best I can with what God blessed me with. You mean to tell me that if you were in my situation, you wouldn't use it to your advantage?"

"I prefer to sleep at night than to live a lie. I know what it's doing to you, and frankly, I don't like it."

"Say hi to Ma'dear for me and tell her that I'll see her next time."

Stella stood in front of the store, watching her only brother walk away. She yelled, "You're breaking her heart, you know?" Julian ignored her and quickly ran toward the car. Chloe's eyes followed the stranger as he walked around to the driver's side. He opened the car door, while he reached in his pocket to take out the bottle of aspirin.

"Hey, I thought you were going to sit up the front with me?" Anyway, the pharmacist said that this wouldn't harm the baby. Although he said that two would be okay to take, I suggest one. What's wrong? Are you okay? Do you feel nauseous?"

"Who was that?" Chloe demanded.

"We better get going before it gets dark."

"No!" She stopped him from putting the key in the ignition. "Who was that, Julian? I thought you weren't from around here."

Julian stared at the steering wheel and then looked at Chloe. "Okay, she's my sister."

"Your sis...ter? Why in God's name is your sister a Colored?"

"I was going to tell you, I swear. I was trying to find a way." He paused for what seemed like an eternity. He then looked out the window, not daring to look her way. And then he began:

"My mother worked for this white family for five years. One day, her husband got sick from pneumonia and almost died. His wife couldn't handle it, so she stayed with her sister and left my mother to take care of him. My mother stayed with him the whole time, and through her nursing him, they fell in love. When she got him on his feet, he bought her a small house. He would visit her every now and again, and through those visits, I was conceived. When his wife found out about the pregnancy, she let my mother go.

"After I was born, her husband, my father, insisted on raising me. He felt that he could give me a better life than my mother could because I was white-looking and all. His wife didn't like it, but she went along with it anyway. As time grew, the woman who I thought was my mother couldn't stand the stares and rumors of people around town. People knew that I wasn't adopted. They knew the truth. She insisted that we move from Mississippi, some place far, far away. So, the bank my dad worked for transferred him to the New York branch. The two of them were all I've ever known. When my father was dying, he told me about my real mother."

"Oh, dear God." Chloe said, in shock.

"He told me everything, while my mother stood in the doorway and wept. Eventually, I sought out my real mother and have kept in touch with her ever since. I vowed to take care of her and my sister if they promised to never reveal my identity."

"So, why are you living a lie? Why are you doing this to me—to yourself, for that matter?"

"You think this is easy for me?"

"Apparently so."

"No, you don't understand. I can't live like a Colored. Just look at them. Do you honestly believe that they can become somebody? And even if they did manage to avoid the minutiae in life, a white man would do everything in his power to knock them back down to size. I've seen it done firsthand in my line of business. I even had to myself."

"I can't do this." She tried to leave the car, but he pulled her arm.

"You can't do what? Haven't I given you the best life any man could possibly give a woman? You don't want for anything."

"But it's a lie!"

"So what?!"

"So what?! So what?!"

"Please, Chloe. I love you, and I know you love me, too. Can't we just work through this? You know now. There are no more secrets."

"No! You lied to me. This is a lie. You've deceived me, just like your parents deceived you when you were growing up. When will it stop?"

"Now. It stops now."

"How can I trust you?"

"By giving me a chance to make it up to you. Please don't walk away from what we've built together. We're married, for crying out loud."

"I thought I was married to a white man. Now I don't know who I'm married to. I don't even know who you are." She tried to leave once more, but he held her back again.

"You can't do this. You're pregnant with our child."

"And what if this child of ours turns out to be your sister's color, huh? What will you do then?" He didn't answer. "Answer me! Will you disown your child?" Will you give it up the way your mother gave you up?" He slapped her so hard that her head hit the window.

"That's not fair!" he screamed.

She looked at him with her hand cradling her face. "How dare you put your hand on me?"

"Please, Chloe. I'm sorry. I'll never do that again. I'm ready this time."

Her face turned as white as a cumulus cloud. Her brown eyes got bigger. "What do you mean, 'this time'?"

He paused. "I mean, I'm not afraid like the last time. I'm ready to face whatever."

She began beating him like a wild woman, punching him and screaming. "How could you?! How could you?! How could you?!"

"No, Chloe stop it." He finally grabbed a hold of her flailing hands and brought her toward him. Chloe made a strange noise— between a cry and a moan. "You told me that it would help me with my headaches. You said that it wouldn't harm the baby. What did you give me before?"

"I just had the pharmacist in the past double whatever was prescribed. I couldn't take the chance of that baby being Colored. I couldn't bear the thought of losing you."

"What do you mean?

"If the baby was to come out Colored, then naturally they'd believe that you had it by a Black man—naturally." Julian said with determined affirmation. "But then, I couldn't put you through that, so I decided to get rid of it. But this time, I'm ready to face whatever..."

"You bastard!" she screamed, "I never want to see you again!"

"Don't say that. You don't mean that. We're married."

"Well, as far as I'm concerned, our marrying is against the law."

"No, I'm a white man in the eyes of the law, and I'm still Julian in your eyes. I'm still the same person you fell in love with."

"So I just complete your whole package, don't I?" Chloe exclaimed.

"Would it have made a difference if I'd told you the truth from the beginning?"

She didn't answer.

"I thought so."

"That's not fair."

"Damn it, Chloe. You wouldn't have given me a second thought. Face it, you're just as racist as the rest of these Ofays out here."

"Don't try to turn this around. You're the one with the sordid past. You're the one who's deceived me. You know what you are? A big phony, a fake, and I never want to see you again."

"Wait, what do you mean?"

"It means that I can find my way back to New York." She fumbled her way out of the car and tried to run. He climbed out of the driver's seat, running after her, yelling. "You can't do this to me. I won't allow it! Chloe, get back here!"

"No. Leave me alone!"

He grabbed her, and they both ended up in the middle of the street. She tried to release herself from his grip. Feeling successful, she yelled out, "Help! Help!"

Everyone in earshot rallied toward the hysterics. Cars stopped in the middle of the street. People got out of their cars to see the disturbance.

"Chloe, you're making a spectacle." Julian said fearfully.

Not listening, "This man is an imposter, a fake. He deceived me into marriage." She cried.

"Please don't do this. You don't understand what they'll do to me."

"He made me love him, marry him, and now I'm pregnant with his Nigger baby."

Everyone looked in sheer puzzlement. They, too, wondered what she was talking about. Some murmurs and whispers ensued, with folks asking the question, "Isn't that the Clemenses' daughter?"

He tried reaching to her, "Get your hands off me. This man that stands before you is not a white man, but a Colored! He's been passing as white. He's been passing!"

Everyone was stunned, especially Julian. He was cemented in shock. He could not believe that the woman he loved and with whom he shared everything had just told the entire town that he was passing for white. Anger blanketed the onlookers. Suddenly, a rock was thrown from out of the crowd, and then another, until Julian was pitched at with a horde of stones, and sticks, and hate. Chloe came to herself and tried to rescue her husband from the hungry mob. She pleaded for them to stop, but her pleas were drowned by the hisses and slanderous remarks.

"Get that Nigger!" someone yelled.

"Hang 'im high!" cried another

"We ain't gonna tolerate no imposters," yelled another voice.

Chloe knew what was next and tried to use her body to cover her husband, who was being beaten, kicked, and spat on by the racist mob. A man reached down and pulled Chloe, but she bit him on the hand. He yelled and smacked her across the face. She fell to the ground. The sheriff drove through the chaos, followed by a dusty red-and-white pick-up truck. The crowd peeled, while the men made their way through.

"Go on now," commanded the sheriff. "Leave him be." To one onlooker, "What in tarnation is going on here?"

"Them young folks are married, and that man is a Colored!" said one spectator.

The sheriff began to case the situation. In his scope, he spotted Chloe. "Oh, you the Clemens child? You the one who rose up and went up north ain't ya?"

Chloe tried to collect herself. "Somebody get her a handkerchief to wipe her mouth." A woman handed her a piece of cloth. Chloe looked at her gratefully and tried her best to answer the sheriff.

"Yes, sir. I need to get him to a hospital, and then we're going home."

"Well, I reckon I can't let you do that."

"Why not?"

"Somebody said that this man is a Negra and the two of you are married?" The sheriff spat out a wad of tobacco juice. "That there is against the law in these parts. You know that, Miz Chloe?"

"Please Sheriff Tanner, I'll do anything. Just let him go. We'll leave Mississippi and never come back."

"We gonna take care of this matter once and for all," Tanner said.

A loud cry was heard from the crowd. It was Stella, running toward her brother's side.

"How could you do this?" Stella yelled to Chloe. "How could you let this happen? You couldn't stand to be humiliated, but now you see the consequences and you're sorry and want to take him home? Well, as far as I'm concerned, his home isn't with you either." She turned to her brother. "How could you let this happen? You know you can't trust these people around here. I'm taking you home, right now." She tried lifting her brother onto his feet. He wobbled a bit but was able to get himself together.

"Hold it, now," said Sheriff Tanner. "This boy can't go with neither one of you. He's gotta be locked up 'til we can get this whole debacle straight."

"I mean, does it have to come to that? Why can't I just take him home?" Stella asked. "Look, Sheriff Tanner, you've known my family a long time, and we've never given any of you just cause to be upset with us. Please, he's my brother. He never meant any harm. He just met someone in New York and fell in love."

Sheriff Tanner chimed into her speech. "He's a Negra, and a white person being married to a Negra is unlawful." He turned his head and spat once more. "Listen here, gal, it ain't personal. I'm just doin' what's right. Deputy," he motioned, "take this man in."

The deputy hastily ran over to Julian and cuffed him from behind. Stella released him into the hands of the law.

"Julian, I'm so sorry." Chloe said, with eyes filled tears.

Julian looked up from his unbeaten eye, half-conscious, and said, "No, I'm sorry, Chloe."

Chloe cried while the man she loved was seized and taken away. Stella slapped Chloe. She realized that she could be taken away along with her brother for putting her hands on a white person. When it seemed that the present incident was on the verge of escalation, Chloe put her hand up to surrender the fight, shook her head toward the sheriff, and ran to her car. The sting of Stella's bold, callous, and convicting blow made Chloe feel sorry about her impetuous outburst toward the only man she had ever loved. While these thoughts ran through her mind, her headache started up again. She slid in the backseat and drifted off into a slow, deep sleep.

The next morning, Chloe was awakened by a rap on her car window. She'd been parked on the street all night. Stella was on the other side of the window and made a gesture for her to roll it down.

"Hey, I thought you'd be long gone by now."

"Oh, I guess I fell asleep."

"I tell you what—we both want the same thing. Why don't you come to my house for breakfast and perhaps we can both figure out how to get Danny out of jail. What do you say?"

"Danny?"

"Yes. My brother? Your husband?"

"Don't you mean 'Julian'?"

"Julian. My brother's name is Daniel Wright."

"Why did he change his name?"

"I don't know. My brother's a complete mystery.

"You said it."

"Hey, I know you were angry and all, but why did you have to make a scene? Why couldn't you get this straight someplace else, without the mob? Now I don't know what's happened to him...he could be..."

"Dead?" Her eyes began to well.

"Look, let's not expect the worst. Maybe they're just holding him.

"Yeah, maybe. But I need to see him. I want to take him home."

"Look, before you get my brother, there's someone I'd like you to meet."

Stella handed Chloe a slip of paper with her address written on it. Then she ran across the street. Chloe watched her for a while, and then looked down at the piece of paper. *Who is this?* Chloe was confused and disoriented, but she couldn't blame anyone but herself. She was right. Why did she make such a spectacle? She should have waited and dealt with the situation back home. Now, she has to deal with the consequences of her impetuous behavior.

She gently rubbed her stomach. "I don't have time to sit and chat. I need to get my husband," Chloe said aloud. She started the car and headed down the road. She wanted to go and get her husband, but she was compelled to stop at Stella's. So many questions festered inside her head. She found herself following the address to the letter. *What if it's a trap*? She thought. But still, that didn't stop her from taking the left, and then a right toward Perry Street. Before she could think any more underlying thoughts, she was in front of the home with her mother-in-law, sitting on the porch—waiting. She stopped the car and eased from behind the wheel. She found herself gravitating towards her, and then she paused. Her mother-in-law stood like a cypress tree with her arms folded.

"Well, are you coming up to give your Ma'dear a hug, or do I have to come down there with my bad knees and carryin' on?"

Chloe ran to her like a prodigal child who realized the errors of her ways...or maybe how she longed to be with her own mother, if she'd give her half the chance. Chloe melted into her arms and didn't want to let go. She wanted to stay in this strange-familiar, never to return to the cold reality of her life. Suddenly, Chloe cried.

"I'm sorry, ma'am. I didn't mean for all of this to happen. I was just upset—and hurt—and confused."

"Shhh, chile. Don't upset yourself. You had some help with this messy creation. If only he'd been honest from the beginning." She pulled Chloe from her bosom with both hands on either shoulder. "He wrote me about you. He said that you was the prettiest thing he'd ever seen."

"You're too kind," Chloe said through her tears. "I don't know how to start."

"Well, I can figure 'bout what happened," she exclaimed. "He lied. I knew this day would come. I knew that him passing would turn and bite him on the behind." She laughed full and heartily. Chloe looked at her strangely. She found nothing funny about this situation. The mother continued. "He had the opportunity to come home with me, but he refused; said he was happy with his present situation. I begged him not to mess with God's work. I told him that deceit had no place in the matters of God's plan. He didn't want to hear all that—said he'd continue to write me every day." She sat back down. When she sat, it was like the relief of twenty-five long years was let out of her. She continued, "When he graduated from Yale, I was so proud. I'd like to think that I had a piece to do with it, but in the real of things, I reckon not. I really wanted to see him graduate. But he said that it wouldn't be a good idea if I came because *she* wouldn't know how to explain things.

"I'm sorry..." Chloe paused. "What shall I call you?"

"Just call me 'Ma'Dear.'" She looked at Chloe and stretched her hand out toward her. Chloe reached out and grabbed it. They both smiled at one another, but then concern hovered over Chloe. "I want to see him. I have to see him and bail him out. Do you think that the sheriff will understand if I explained the whole story?"

"Well, there's no sense in asking me. Why don't you go into town and get your husband," she said with encouragement.

"I will. I will get him, and I'm going to bring him back here before we leave for New York."

"I'd like that. I'd like that very much, Chloe."

Chloe leaned into her and gave her a huge hug. Then she whispered in her ear, "Thank you so very much."

>>>

"That damn girl. I can't believe she shamed us this way. Why would she shame us?" Father said. He eased himself down in a chair on the porch, exasperated and confused.

Earlier that evening, Roseanne was so distraught after the dinner with her sister and her husband. She especially hated the way her mother treated her sister. Bill saw his wife-to-be in shambles and suggested they go out to get some air. While driving, they saw a crowd, yelling and screaming obscenities. Bill parked the car and proceeded out. Roseanne pulled him back.

"Bill, what are you doing?"

"Well, I want to see what's going on."

"I don't think it's any of our business. Let's just go for that drive. There's a lot I need to talk about."

"I know, I know, Rosie. Just let me see what's going on and then we can go. Okay?" He didn't wait for her answer but jumped out of the car and hastily walked toward the commotion.

"What's going on?" he asked the first man he encountered.

"Well, there's a Nigger claiming to be white. Turns out, his wife didn't know it either. Ain't that a shit in a storm?"

Bill got closer and saw Chloe covering her husband. "My word." He whispered. He witnessed the angry mob pulling her off him and heard her screaming at the top of her lungs. He was paralyzed. He wanted to go in and help, but his feet were planted. Then the rocks flew, and the objects landed on the body, desperate to find refuge on the ground. He watched as the rocks burst the flesh, blood spilling onto the streets; he peered as sticks pounded the man's flesh, splitting his neck, his shoulder, and his skull. His reflexes lunged forward toward Julian's limp and helpless body.

"Hey Bill, you want some of this?" A man handed him a bloody stick. Bill looked at the stick and turned away to get out of the chaos before the mob put two and two together. He quickly turned around to find Roseanne directly behind him, looking on in tears. They looked at one another, and Bill rushed her off.

"Roseanne, we gotta get outta here before they recognize you."

"She's my sister. I have to go to her. She's my sister."

"Rosie, we can't get mixed up in this. We gotta go and tell your parents."

"But she's my sister...."

Bill grabbed her hand and pulled her from the slaughter. He tightened his grip on her wrist and struggled to pull her to the car. "Rosie, we gotta go." He gently pushed her inside, but like a lone tree with strong roots, she could not be moved.

"This isn't right, Bill. Let's go to her. She needs me. She's my baby sister. I should be the one to protect her." Tears streamed from her eyes. Bill turned her to him and looked into her tear-flooded eyes. He held her in his arms.

"I know, I know. But there's nothing we can do. It's too risky. Maybe we can do something when the smoke clears."

"Smoke clears. Did you see him? He didn't look as if he would survive what they were doing! It's awful! It's awful! Oh, God why!" She fell to her knees, crying out. Bill held her closer. When he got a better grip, he opened the passenger side of the car and eased her inside. Quickly, he shut the door and ran to the driver's side. He revved the engine, made a U- turn, and flew down the road toward Roseanne's home.

"Well, whatever Chloe got is what she deserved. To hell with her!" said Mother and went into the house.

15

"Where is he? Where is my husband?" Chloe's rant disrupted the everyday affairs at the sheriff's office, but she didn't care. "I'm here to see him. Why can't I see him?" The deputy started to open his mouth when Sheriff Tanner walked through the door. She left the deputy and ran to the sheriff.

"Sheriff Tanner, I came to see my husband and to post bail. Where is he?"

"Well, he was a bit hostile. When we went into the holdin' cell to check on him, he just went plain loco and tried to wrestle my deputy to the floor."

She looked at the deputy, while Sheriff Tanner continued to explain what seemed to her to be a ridiculous story.

"That doesn't sound like Julian. He wouldn't do anything like that."

"Darlin', have you ever seen a man in a desperate situation? You don't know what he'll do when his back is against the wall—trapped like a wild animal."

"He's not an animal. He's an intelligent man."

"Well, you didn't seem to think as much when you was rantin' and ravin' 'bout him not being who he said."

"I made a mistake! How many times must I tell you?"

"Once was enough, and what's done is done!" When he noticed a scene building, he lowered his voice. "Now, if you will excuse me, I got more important matters to tend to." He walked away, leaving Chloe baffled.

"Where is he? Will anyone tell me where my husband is? Please, somebody help me." When she realized that no one was on her side, she dashed out of the station. She scurried to her car. Someone was right on her heel. Before she could acknowledge who this person was...

"Get in and drive around the corner—now!" The deputy hurried her into the car. She slid over to the driver's seat. He looked around, before getting in the passenger side. Chloe turned the ignition and peeled off with a screeching noise to the tar.

"Turn right down here," he urged demandingly. She did. "Make a left onto the dirt road." He demanded once more. She obeyed. "This is fine." She slowed down and stopped the car. She turned off the engine. The dirt road overlooked a lake. A huge oak tree served as a hiding place for them. She turned her body toward him; however, the deputy continued looking straight ahead, as if something pulled him to not look to the left or to the right. He began...

"It was awful. I couldn't believe it was happening." The deputy continued his stare out into the lake, as if the action was taking place before his eyes. Chloe was dead set on his mouth—capturing every word that dripped from it. "They didn't have to do it." A tear fell from his eye. Chloe was frightened. She had an idea what the outcome was but was intent on knowing how. "It was about 2 a.m. when two men stormed into his cell where he slept and dragged him out. He asked them what was going on, but one of the men demanded him to—

"'Shut up! Just shut up!'

"'I demand to know where you're taking me. I have a right to know.'

"'Boy, the only rights you have is... well, you have none,' one of the men said."

"Both men laughed as they dragged him toward a red-and-white dusty pick-up truck."

"'Will you two dipsticks shut up?' Sheriff Tanner said. "'And where's that deputy? He's supposed to be helping with this.'

"'I think he's afraid,' I heard one of the men say.

"'Yeah,' the first one chimed in. "'You know how them Canadians are?'

"'Well, he's in Mississippi now, and he's gotta learn how things is done 'round here.'

"Next thing I knew, Sheriff Tanner was approaching me—coaxing me to come along. He said that it was my God-given duty as an American and that we shouldn't let some Nigger perpetrate and take our women away."

Chloe hung on to the deputy's every word. Her eyes did not deviate from his moving mouth. The deputy continued the story in a low, dry voice.

"With some threatening of my job and my life, I joined them. I didn't sign up for this. I...we drove for what seemed like an hour out of the way. Your husband was tied and gagged in the back of the truck. Everyone was excited, including the sheriff. I was so scared. When we arrived to the destined spot, they dragged him off the bed of the truck like an animal. They didn't bother to untie him, and when I reached for the rope, one of the men put a shotgun to my head."

"'If you touch him, I'll shoot you dead.'

"Shouldn't he be...?'

"'Leave him be,' said the sheriff. 'He don't know how it's done.'

"'Then he said to me,"

'Consider this my initiation.'

"'String 'im up,' he ordered."

"The two men did just that. He dangled helplessly by the wrists and was tied to the branch of an oak tree."

"'Pull down his pants,' the sheriff said, and this time he was looking at—

'Me?'

"I cried a bit. I refused as long as I could, but Tanner told me that if I didn't do what he said, I would be strung up beside him. So I did."

"'That's a good boy', he said to me. 'Now, take this knife and cut off his thing.'

"Everyone laughed. I couldn't pull myself together. I couldn't believe what I was hearing and what they wanted me to do. He shoved the knife in my hand. I held my hand up, but I shook so badly that I couldn't hold the knife steady. I couldn't concentrate with the screaming from your husband. He begged through the gag for me not to do it. This became more hilarious to the men."

"'Do it!' he yelled."

"I raised the knife and then dropped it. I just couldn't do it. I begged the sheriff, pleaded with him, even. I told him that this was wrong. What they...we were doing was wrong."

"'Get out of my way, you sissy.'

"He took the knife out of my hand. "'Worthless,'" he said under his breath. He raised his hand to heaven and, in one swoop, cut it off."

"'A clean sweep.'

"He went into a spasmodic seizure and passed out. Foam raced from out of the gag and onto the side of his cheek. He shook so violently that he broke the branch he hung from and crashed to the ground."

"'Damn it, this is messing everything up. Try waking him up. I want him awake for the burning.'

"One of the men tried waking him by slapping his face, but it was no use. By this time, blood was pooling from everywhere..."

"Oh God!" Chloe cried.

"Well ma'am, aren't you the one who cried that your husband was an imposter?

It seemed to me that you'd be..." He caught himself, realizing that he was on the verge of perverse insensitivity.

"Are you saying that I wanted this to happen to my husband? I was upset. I didn't know what I was saying." She paused.   Then a gut-wrenching scream resounded out of her, startling the deputy.

He looked at her for a moment, and then pulled her close so that she could lean on him. This, in a way, was good for him, too, for he had witnessed the horrific sighting of a real, live lynching. He'd only heard about them through stories his mother had told him. He didn't actually think they were true. He thought that she told the "tall tales" to keep him home. He was a man—or so he felt—and wanted to move as far away from the deadbeat town as possible. "Where the action is—that's where I belong," he boasted back home. So when the South came a-callin', he went a-runnin'. "But I didn't expect anything such as the likes of this. I guess my mom was right."

"'Keep going, deputy.'"

"'He ordered me to get the gasoline out of my trunk. 'I'm ready to torch this Negra.'

"He turned his back to the whole situation. 'I'm gettin' bored.'

"One of the men looked strangely at the sheriff, for he thought that the comment was disheartening. But then again, he was a cold-hearted crazy man. 'What the hell you lookin' at?' he continued. 'Get the damn gasoline 'for there's two bonfires!'

"The other man arrived with the gasoline. He shook the can until the clear liquid was released, streaming onto the unfortunate soul. By this time, he woke up. I guess it was the fumes that did it. And, through his gag, we all heard a muffled scream. This amused the three men."

"'Fry 'im,' he said in a low tone."

And with that, a torch was lit and the body slowly burned from head to toe. His screams became louder and more pronounced from the torture and unprecedented pain.

That night, Daniel was in the clutches of hell, and its origin was the devil.

16

He walked alone along the wide pond that surrounded the wooded area just five miles from his home. He'd decided to do this last night, after the fight between his mom and dad, followed by his father's demise. He wanted to leave then; however, he was paralyzed by the body that he heard hurling against the wall three times consecutively. There are certain things you cannot control as an eight-year-old—where to sleep, what to eat, and the parents that God chains you to. Although the former two can be regulated with some adjustments, the last is inevitable, no matter how hard we try as adults to suppress, hide, or cover our genetic inheritance.

At any rate, he waited for the quiet and then pushed himself out of his bed and ran to the kitchen as fast as his little fat feet could carry him. He grabbed a towel and held it under the cold water. The water ran on the towel, some soaking into the towel, while the remainder ran into the sink, down the drain, to try again. He held it there and held it there. He didn't move. He couldn't move. All he could hear was the one...two...three body slams against the wall and the fourth, hitting the floor.

He came to. He turned off the water, wrung out the towel, and ran toward his parents' bedroom. He saw the door slightly ajar and slowed his pace. He hated this part. With his little fat hand, he eased the door open to find his mother on the floor, bloody and battered. Her arm was behind her back, as if it were detached from her body. Her greasy blonde hair covered her face. He followed the blood trail toward her. She was out cold. He walked slowly toward his out-cold mother and bent down in front of her. He reached out his little fat hand to brush the hair from her face, afraid to find the worse-than-usual on it.

"Leave her be," said a voice, low and shaky.

He jumped up and saw his father. He was hurt too. A knife handle stuck out from his chest, with the blade stuck just above his heart. The boy forgot about his mother and walked toward his father, slumped against the wall with his legs sprawled like a rag doll.

"Yeah, she really got me this time, boy. I didn't know she had it in her. I didn't know she had that knife." He chuckled.

The boy bent down and stuck out his little fat hand and touched the handle of the knife that stuck out of his father's chest, just above his heart.

"Yeah, she really got me this time, J.T.. She's a feisty one, your mother. That's why I love her. She knows how to surprise a fella." He coughed and smarted and groaned because with every pressure, the blade squeezed and pinched his chest. He looked down and saw the blood oozing from his chest. "Damn it." He said lightly. J.T. watched his father for a bit and then shoved the knife farther into his chest, twisting it and turning it. His father screamed and tried to reach for his wayward son's arm, but the pain was too great. He managed, however, to grab his shirt to pull him closer.

J.T. held on tighter to the handle, and the knife plunged farther into his chest. His father's eyes widened, and he slumped to one side on the floor. There was a *snap,* and J.T. was holding the handle in his hand, with the blade still stuck in his father's chest. He was dead. J.T. stayed like that, holding the handle in his hand and watching his father on the floor, bleeding out of his chest. He reached out his fat little hand and closed his father's eyes. He leaned down so that his mouth swept his ear. "Rot in hell, you sonofabitch."

"J.T.?" were his father's last words to his son.

He jumped up and quickly turned to find his mother slightly conscious. Her dirty, greasy blonde hair covered her face. She lightly hoisted herself up with her good arm and tried to move the bad one. She screamed. J.T. rushed to her aid.

"Don't move. Your arm is broken, Momma."

"Shit."

"I gotta call somebody. Daddy's dead."

"Shit."

"I gotta call somebody."

"Call T-bone."

J.T. ran to the phone that hung on the kitchen wall and called his uncle T-bone.

17

Loretta hung the clothes on the line with her older daughter, Terri, in tow. Naomi played with her dolls in the grass. The breeze was just right for an afternoon of washing and hanging. Loretta pulled and tugged at the sheet, wrestling to get it out of the basket. Terri saw her frustration and bent down to loosen the wayward sheet. Terri hurried to help her mother untangle the sheet. She pulled it to her side and hung it at the other end of the clothes wire with a clothespin.

"Momma, you all right?"

"Yes, baby."

"Are you sure?"

Loretta stopped what she was doing and walked toward her daughter. Terri faced her, and her mother put her face in her hands. "I've been so busy with my own issues, I had no idea how this must be affecting you guys."

"It's okay, Momma."

Terri knew what was wrong and why her father was gone. She'd heard them yelling five days earlier about a man named Toby Wallace and how he'd been communicating with Loretta for three months. She also heard her mother crying and her father slamming things around the bedroom, yelling and screaming.

"I'm sick of this. I'm your husband, Retta. How you gonna do this to me?"

"Ray, it's not what you think. My dad is sick, and Toby is his physician. I knew how you felt about my dad, so I didn't bother telling you. But eventually I was going to."

"But I'm your husband. You should have told me from the beginning. Damn, Retta, I'm not a tyrant. I'm not mean. I understand about these things. I lost both my parents. I could have been there for you."

"Could have?"

"You know what I mean. I still can be. But you go behind my back and I find this letter. This ain't got nothin' to do with your daddy." Holding the letter in his hand.

"He...I...I don't know why he wrote that letter. I guess he was feeling some kind of a way and... I don't know why."

"The hell you don't. He's talking about how he couldn't wait to see you and how he misses you and why did you marry somebody like me and he could've given you a better life. A life you deserve. And wanting to know are you happy...?"

"Ray, please."

"Loretta, please! Why would he say those things if you all wasn't communicatin' in that way? So tell me, are you happy? Do I make you happy, or do you feel that you deserve better?"

"Ray, I love you. Don't do this."

Ray was silent. He plopped on the edge of the desk that sat by the window in the bedroom. He didn't know who this woman was. He wished he'd never seen the letter. His mind went back even further to when he came in from work and kissed her on the cheek and flew upstairs to go to the bathroom, and then the bedroom to take off his shoes to lie down before dinner and noticed the mound on the desk and smiled a bit because of his wife's arduous work ethics, and when his baby girl ran in the bedroom and hopped on the bed beside him and lay on his chest and played with his hands and his newly grown beard, and Loretta called her to help set the table, and Naomi running out in obedience....

By accident, she knocked over the pillow on her mother's side of the bed, and Ray spotted the letter that read "To: Loretta" in cursive on the front of the envelope and picked it up and saw a name on the top left hand corner of the envelope that read, "Toby Wallace," and what looked like his personal address in Louisiana. And Ray picked up the envelope and opened it and saw a letter inside that read, "To Loretta," and then he read on and found himself getting angrier and angrier. And then Loretta came upstairs and found her husband's back turned on his side of the bed, slightly bent over. And she found that her pillow was on the floor and the letter missing—but no, not missing; it was in Ray's hand. He was reading the letter and turned around with his eyes welling and his lip tight, and Loretta was disquieted and panicky.

"Retta, we've always been straight with one another. We've always told each other the truth, no matter how much it bruised." He braced himself, "Are you sorry you married me?"

"No. I mean, sometimes it's hard. Sometimes I wonder what I would have done had I finished school. But I've never wondered what it would've been like with someone else. I knew the choice I made. I knew what I was getting into..."

Loretta stood there trying to convince her husband of seventeen years that it was not what he thought. And Ray, who knocked over more things and plopped on the edge of the bed, held his head in his hands. Loretta, who sat beside him, rubbed the back of his head and kissed his cheek and the tear that finally rolled from his right eye. And Ray, who held her hand, couldn't look in her face just yet and put on his shoes and walked out of the room. Loretta called for her husband of seventeen years and ran after him and saw him get into his truck. She cried in the evening air and fell to her knees, and called out to Ray, who drove off because he was in so much pain. And the children ran out to their mother and held her and comforted her and brought her inside. This is what Terri heard. This is what she saw.

"No, it's not okay. It's never okay for children to see their parents going through this kinda stuff. Thing is, I just don't know..." Loretta hung her head down with a feeling of shame. She was supposed to have it all together for her children, especially her daughters. But the thing was, she didn't have it all together. She didn't know what she was doing. She was all mixed up. Confused. Exasperated. Disjointed.... Terri saw her fragmented state and fell into her mother's arms, pressing her head into her chest. Loretta obliged her daughter's desperation and held her close.

"Momma...are you and Daddy....?" She started to cry in her mother's chest. Loretta held her tighter because she knew what her question was. However, she wasn't ready to answer or more important, didn't know what to answer. So, she just held her daughter tighter, tears streaming down her face, into her daughter's hair.

18

It was late afternoon when Ray brought Tiger home. Tiger was laden with hurt and deepened with pain.   He was distraught at the idea of his and his father's argument, when he came in to find him in the presence of another woman. He was also saddened at the fact that he had to break it off with Maybelle. He could not risk his life for one silly adventure, no matter how strange, how intriguing, or how beautiful it was. He needed to think of his future. He had to be the strong one. Besides, wasn't she leaving when summer ended? Then what would happen? He would be caught up and then dumped. He probably would never see her again. And the way his family was headed, he knew seeing her again was highly unlikely.

But that didn't matter now. The first time he'd ever fallen for someone and not only was she not from here, but she was white. He wanted to know that love still worked. He wanted to know, when you fall in love, was it for life? It certainly didn't seem that way for his parents. They were splitting up, and there was nothing he could do about it. But if he made it work in his own life, maybe….

"Tiger, I'm sorry about what happened back there at the store." Ray broke Tiger's thoughts. By this time, he was standing on the passenger side. Tiger didn't notice when the truck stopped or when his father got out of the truck and walked to the side where he was. Tiger looked at him but didn't say a word. He continued, "I know it was strange about what you saw, but I never cheated on your mother, and I never will. I love your mother. The whole visit was…." Ray's voice trailed off.

Tiger needed to tell him about Maybelle. He needed to know how he could be with her. He needed to know because he was in love with her. He wanted to run away with her, but that, he knew, was out of the question. However, when he graduated next year, he would be able to do whatever he wanted, and he wanted to go up north and be with Maybelle. That was his plan, but he had to talk to his father. He needed to know if love really worked.

"...you understand son?"

"Dad, I have something to tell you."

"What?"

"Unh? I'm sorry, Dad, but I need to talk."

"I thought we were talking."

"I have to tell you something."

Ray got closer to Tiger, who still sat in the truck. Tiger fumbled with a piece of torn vinyl on the seat where he sat. The dingy white stuffing showed, but as he pulled and fumbled more, more vinyl loosened and new stuffing was revealed, showing it to be whiter than the old and dingy stuffing.

"What is it son?"

He looked up from his project and into his father's eyes. They began to well. "I...I met someone."

"Okay."

"Dad, she's white. Her name is Maybelle. I met her one day while I was on my way to see you. She was standing outside Mr. Simms's store. She's his niece and..."

"Them folks are the meanest and the most racist people this side of Mississippi. I can't have you mixed up in all of this."

"Dad, that's not all. I love her and she loves me."

"You think you do. Come on, Tiger, there are plenty of beautiful colored girls around town. Why you gotta go and mess with the one you forbidden to have?"

"Dad, it wasn't like I was looking for it. She was just standing there and..."

"And what, Tiger?"

"I just knew."

"You just knew?"

"Well, yeah."

"How?"

"What do you mean, 'How'? Like anybody else would know when they meet their soulmate."

"So, you believe that that white girl is your soulmate?"

"Why do you have to say it like that?" Besides, does it matter her color? I mean, you told me that when you saw mom at that juke joint years ago, standing against the wall, you knew right away."

"Your mom and me are different."

"Why, Dad? Because you two are the same color? So you're saying that if Maybelle was Colored and I was telling you this story, you would be patting me on the back by now. But because she's white then it's not the same? Does love have a color?"

"What? Of course not, but you can't go around thinking that it's okay to be with a white girl, either. I don't care where she's from."

"Well, I broke it off with her. I told her what you just said."

"Well, all right. Did anyone see you two together?

"I don't know. I don't think so…."

"You can't see her again. You can get killed doing that. Don't you know that?"

"But Dad, that's the thing. I don't want to stop seeing her. I want to be with her. I was thinking that when I graduate next year, instead of going to college around here, I could go up north. Then we can be together freely."

"The hell, you think this is a fairytale?" You are colored and she is white. When you go up north, you'll still be colored and she will still be white. It doesn't matter. You cannot commingle with those people. Colored men have gotten themselves killed, thinking that they can defy the laws of Crow."

"But we'll be up north...."

"It don't matter. Crow is Crow, no matter where you go."

Tiger sat back in his seat and rested his head back. He didn't like what his father said, but he knew he was right. He knew that it was a dead end. He turned and looked at him.

"How long you and Mom going to keep this up?"

"Keep what up?"

"Come on, Dad."

"Yeah, son. I'm going to..." Before he could get out what he was about to say, he felt something tugging on his shirt. He looked down and it was Naomi, staring at him with her big brown eyes.

"You coming inside, Daddy?"

"Hey, Naopoloy. How are you? He picked her up, and she wrapped her little arms around his neck.

"I miss you, Daddy," she whispered in his ear.

Ray felt his heart flutter.

"Dad, why don't you go inside and resolve this thing with Mom, please?"

He looked at his son and then at his daughter. He put her down and did an about-face toward the house. Tiger got out of the car and grabbed Naomi by the hand to take her inside. When Ray reached the screen door, he opened it wide and let it slam behind him, as he usually did when he came home. Loretta knew it was him because she had watched the whole time from the bedroom window. She witnessed

Tiger and Ray talking. She saw Naomi run outside to greet her father and saw him pick her up. She saw when he turned to walk into the house.

A smile grew from the corners of her full mouth. She missed her husband of seventeen years. She couldn't function while he was away. She sat and stewed and missed three days of work. She stayed in the house, while Terri took over the household, while Tiger tried to coax his father to come home because he knew what bad shape his mother was in. But now he was home and they could be a family again.

19

"I did it, T-bone. I killed him. Just like we talked about."

"Hush, boy. You want dem cops to hear you? As far as you concerned, your momma was defending herself, and when you walked in, he was already dead."

"But my prints...they on the handle." He opened his hand to reveal the handle from the knife. "See, I still have it."

"Gimme that, boy." He snatched the knife handle from him and quickly put it in his back pocket. "Look, you ain't done nothin' wrong. You's innocent. As far as you concerned, your momma was defending herself against that sumbitch, hear?"

"Yes sir."

"Yeah, he got what he deserved. He took advantage of your momma for far too long, using his power for evil."

"They both did."

"Don't speak ill 'bout your momma. She didn't know no better."

The coroner rolled J.T.'s father out of the bedroom on a stretcher. T. Bone and J.T. were sitting at the kitchen table. The light was dim. J.T. watched his father being rolled out of the house with a white sheet covering him and blood seeping through it. It all seemed as if he were watching someone else's life. He stared at his father being rolled out of the house and put in the back of a long black car that was made to carry dead bodies. He was transfixed on the two men sliding his father's body into the car.

A voice broke J.T.'s trance. "Are you okay?"

"Where y'all takin 'im?"

"The morgue. What happened here, J.T.? I know you're a bit shaken up right now, but I'm gonna really need you to—."

"Come on now, Randy. Ain't the boy been through enough for one night? Lay off 'til mornin'."

The deputy looked down at J.T., still looking out the door to where his father was being taken away by the coroners.

"Yeah, I guess you're right. We'll just take a statement tomorrow morning. See to it that he's brought down to the station. Bright and early, eh T-Bone?"

"Yeah, sure. Whatever." T-Bone was staring at J.T..

"Shit. People ain't gonna take too kindly to the sheriff being knifed up by his old lady. Come on, boys. Let's go back to the station. Ain't nothin' to be done around here tonight." He looked down at J.T. "Get some rest and go see your momma in the morning." J.T. didn't answer. He was still transfixed on the evening.

"Hey, deputy. I can't find the handle," a voice called from the bedroom.

"Whatdaya mean you 'can't find it'?" He turned to look at T-Bone and then at J.T. "Sheriff Tanner had a blade stuck in his chest, without the handle attached. Do y'all know anything about this?"

"Hey..." T- Bone interjected, "I thought y'all was gonna wait 'til the morning. Ain't he been through enough shit tonight?"

The deputy looked at T-Bone long and hard. "Yeah..." He turned his focus on J.T. "Bright and early." And with that, the deputy motioned for his crew with a side nod of his head, and off they proceeded out of the house and into the squad cars.

20

Tiger rolled over in his bed early the next morning. He heard the birds chirping outside his window. He lay there, looking up at the ceiling. He had to see her. He couldn't stay away from her. He thought about what his dad had said yesterday evening. He knew the consequences, but that still didn't negate the fact that he wanted to, needed to see her. He had to touch her creamy white face, intertwine his fingers in hers, while she laid her head on his shoulder and he recited the poem to her once again, this time saying the whole thing. He wanted to tell her that he loved her and that he would be with her for sure next year, when he finished school. He needed to be next to her so that he could breathe again... feel again... smile again... want again.

So he got up and went into the bathroom to wash up. He thought about Maybelle and how it could work. He needed to tell her that there was a solution and that they could be together after all. He knew he left her in lather, but he could apologize and kiss her lips and tell her to hold tight until he got up north. For her not to be restless and want or need for another, but to only pine for him until they were back in each other's arms.

The more he thought about this destined union, the quicker he moved. He ran back to his room, put on his clothes and shoes, and ran down the stairs toward the front door. It was around eight Saturday morning, and he hoped that she would be at the store, standing outside the way she always did, secretly waiting for him.

"Where you going?"

"Mom, I didn't see you there."

"Yes, I'm here. What are you doing up so early in the morning?"

"I…uh…have something that I have to take care of."

"Like what?"

"I…"

"Before you go into some kind of a lie, your father told me how you were spending your time and who you were spending it with. Is that where you're going?"

Tiger froze. He was speechless. He couldn't think fast enough. He knew he needed to see her.

"Mom, it's okay. I just want to see her before she goes back home. I want to tell her goodbye."

"Why are you doing this? It's not safe. You know how Mississippi is? Why are you doing this?"

"Mom, please. Is this why you're up, to tell me that I'm making a mistake and that I can't see Maybelle anymore?"

"No, I mean...I was up, but here you are..."

"You and Dad are...where is Dad?"

"Upstairs. We talked. I'll be leaving for Louisiana this evening. My father, your grandfather, is sick, and I need to take care of him."

"Really? How come we never saw him or visited him?"

"Because he didn't accept your father, or me for that matter. Your father and I left and got married, and then we came here to take over the store his father left him before he died."

"Why didn't he accept dad or you? You're his daughter."

"He had his expectations for me and I clearly did not follow them. I was pregnant with you when I told my father. I was a junior in college, and he had someone else for me, but I chose your father. I had to. I..."

"Loved him?"

"Yes. I still do. I never stopped."

"I love *her,* Mom."

"Tiger, please, think about what you're doing."

He bent down to where his mother sat in the chair by the window. Before he flew down the stairs, she was already up. She sat by the bed where her husband lay. She looked at him for a long while and then put her robe on to go downstairs to the kitchen to make a pot of coffee. They talked all night and into the morning. She told him that Toby had been writing her for the past three years because her father had taken ill. She was living vicariously through Toby. She wanted very much to see her father, but she knew she couldn't bring herself to. So, she communicated with Toby through letters.

The letter that Ray found was the beginning of Toby being forward. He was not professional nor considerate. He did not explain that the cancer was spreading throughout her father's body. He did not explain how he'd talked to his other colleagues about what to do about his brain cancer. He did not explain in the letter that her father refused treatment and how he was alone because her mother had left him three years ago, complaining that she'd had it up to here with his evil and inconsiderate ways, and for him to keep quiet and not tell their daughter. He did not allude to the fact that his father had to stop working and went crazy in his head because he told Toby that it sounded like bugs were crawling through his brain. He did not have the heart to tell her that her father had died shortly after because he heard the bugs crawling in his brain again and that his head was also splitting with pain and he needed to feel relief.

So he reached in the drawer of the nightstand beside his bed and blew his brains out. He could not fathom telling her that her father was long gone and that going to Louisiana would only be in vain because very few people showed up at his funeral, and his wife of twenty-five years didn't bother showing up. But instead, he told her that he wanted to see her and that he wanted to be with her because he never got over her. He said that he could show her the world because he was a surgeon, and that he could give her a big house that would sit alongside the water. They could get married and live happily ever after.

"I will...I have...I just need to take a walk to clear my head."

"Don't you want some breakfast? I can make you some pancakes."

"I'm not hungry."

"Tiger?"

"Yes, Mom?"

"You're unique. You've always been a fighter, a protector. You remind me of your grandfather—intelligent, passionate, and a bit impetuous at times, like now. I don't know what I'd-a done without you this past week. To be without the one you love feels like your soul has taken flight."

Tiger was on one knee at his mother's feet. She looked into his eyes and rubbed his cheek. She brought his face to hers and kissed him.

"If you gotta go, you gotta go. But be careful."

"Yes, mom. I will." And with that, he walked out the door, not knowing that watching her son walk out that door could be her last.

21

Maybelle had defied her mother since the day she was born. She was supposed to be born on September 20th but didn't greet the world until a week later. She tortured her mother, being inside of her. When she was born, she came out dark with white hair. Chloe knew that she would be black like her grandmother. The nurses and doctor looked at her strangely. They immediately put her in another wing of the hospital and told her that she and her Nigger baby had to leave. Chloe had no time to recover but had to pack up and leave with her newborn in her hand. She dragged herself down the street. She didn't even have time to nurse her, let alone name her. Chloe walked five miles home. By the time she reached the stairs she collapsed. When she woke up, a woman was looking in her face. Everything was blurry. She immediately looked around for her baby.

"She's all right. I fed her, and she's sound asleep now."

"Where am I?"

"You're in my home. I'm Leanne. I live up the street from you."

"I...how?"

"I saw you collapse with that baby in your arms. Did you just have that baby?"

"Yes. Yesterday."

"And they released you already?"

"Well, didn't you see her? They thought she was some kind of a freak. Doesn't she look freakish to you?"

Leanne walked over to where the baby lay. "No, she looks like an angel."

"No, she looks like a freak. She's dark with white hair. She'll be colored for sure, and then I'm going to have to move out of my apartment because they don't allow Coloreds where I live. I don't know what I'm gonna do."

"I don't know? My uncle married this Colored woman and they had a son. The son was as white as a sheet when he was born, but as he got older, he turned out as black as a tea kettle. Who knows, maybe your baby girl could do the opposite and you wouldn't have to move."

"Ain't you gonna throw me out because of her?"

"Look, honey, I'm white, and I'm old. I've been on this earth long enough to witness the evils that men do. I was married to a Colored man when I lived in Florida. He was acting like my handyman, and he had a room out in the shed. We lived like that for four years, until one day someone saw us kissing in the backyard. I don't know. I just wanted him to be my husband, not pretend to be a handyman. He went out one day and never returned. I knew something went wrong. I found him two days later. I had to cut him down from a tree three miles up the road from my house."

Leanne sat and stared at the bright colors on the quilt that covered Chloe. The floral, clear stitching that puffed the fabric made the quilt look separated in some areas. She leaned over and touched the quilt. "We'd wrap ourselves in this quilt some mornings, drinking coffee, talking and laughing at whatever. I left Florida soon after and came here to live. People are no different. Geography just a bit closer, that's all."

"I'm sorry..."

"Please, that was long ago. Where's your husband...?"

>>>

When Maybelle got older, she was more defiant. She asked her mother constantly why everyone had a father but her. Not getting a definitive answer from her mother made her more defiant and more determined to be a wayward daughter. It was even truer when her mother had her episodes of depression. Some days, she didn't get out of bed. Maybelle had to go at it alone for days, sometime weeks at a time.

Chloe didn't want to go there, but her mind wouldn't let her do otherwise. Anything could trigger it: a song, a smell, a thought....anything. She became quiet, and then withdrawn. She'd turn all the lights off in the apartment, turn down the shades, crawl into bed, and sleep. Maybelle was used to it and became very good at sensing when the episodes darkened their home. At five, she would sit by her mother's bed and watch her sleep. She didn't know what to do. She did, however, learn quickly—to eat, to walk to school on her own, to take care of herself, to be alone. She learned very fast. She had to, or she would end up like her.

When she got older, she discovered things—like the way her golden blonde hair brushed around her shoulders and how to twirl it around her index finger to lure the attention she desired, and how round and firm her breasts had gotten, along with the roundness and firmness of her hips and behind. And when she walked, how they swayed in a sultry, hypnotic fashion. She further discovered how her facial features differed from a pure white person's. And although her hair was blonde, her lips were full; and although her eyes were blue, her nose was slightly wide. She asked her mother about these awkward features, but she waved her off and told her that God made everyone different. She also noticed the opposite sex, and how to spin tales and lure them into a trap that had the potential to damage.

"So you call yourself Maybelle?"

"Yes."

"I'm Arnold. But my friends call me Arnie."

"Can I call you Arnie?"

"You wanna be my friend?"

"Sure."

His smile widened. "You sure are pretty, Maybelle."

"Thank you."

"Where you going?"

"Home."

"You in school, Maybelle?"

"Yes."

"Are you?"

"Naw. Stayed away from it."

"Why? Everybody needs school."

"Not me. Besides, I never liked school. And it never liked me. So, I stayed away. We got along just fine."

She laughed. "You're funny."

"You sure do have a pretty laugh. So, let's say we go somewhere and get better acquainted?"

"Okay."

"You drink?"

"Sure."

"Yeah, I love a girl who does."

They walked a little ways. He pulled out a pint of whiskey from his back pocket and took a drink.

"You don't mind?"

"Mind what?"

"You know? About my color?" He wiped the top of the bottle and passed it her way.

"I don't if you don't." She took a swig and coughed and coughed.

"You sure you drink?" He chuckled. She smiled and wiped her mouth. He continued, "Well, I've never been with a white girl before. You ever been with a Colored?"

"Sure, plenty of times."

"Plenty?"

"Well…not plenty, but I ain't afraid if that's what you mean?"

"Yeah, that's what I mean. People are people, right?"

"Uhuh."

Turned out, people weren't just people at all. A white man saw her lying on the ground. She explained to him what happened and that the boy got rough with her. The man turned red and convinced her to go to the police, and that he would even drive her. Eventually, that poor boy was arrested and went to jail for rape, but not before he was beaten half to death by some very anxious locals.

It went like this: The two of them got to drinking more and more, and she flirted with him something fierce. He got to the point where he just could take it no longer. They kissed, and he wanted more. She unbuttoned her blouse, and they commenced even further. He slowly parted her legs and rubbed in between. She guided his hand to where she wanted him to go. Just when he began to go a bit farther, she grabbed his hand and squeezed it.

"Come on, girl, whatcha doin'?"

"I'm not ready for that."

"What you mean? You was takin' me there."

"What?"

"You know...that means you ready for what's next."

"No. I don't want to. Besides, it's getting late. I gotta go. My momma's probably won--."

"Aww, girl. You gonna leave me like this?" He pointed to his erection.

Staring, "I...gotta go."

"You some kinda tease, ain't you? Well, I don't like that."

"Well, it's gonna have to do cuz I'm leavin'."

"Come on, just one more kiss."

"No, I gotta go. Please, let me go." She pushed him away as he tried to move in, and the more she resisted, the more persistent he became. "Stop it! Stop it! Let go!!" She smacked him hard across the face. Upon reflex, he slapped her back and she hit the ground.

"I knew you was a crazy white bitch." He left her on the ground.

She curled up in a ball and cried. She hated herself and who she was becoming. She wanted to die, just like her mother.

>>>

"How was school today?"

"Please, like you care." Maybelle tried to whisk past her mother but was unsuccessful.

She grabbed her by the arm with one hand and grabbed her face with the other. She discovered a red mark across her face and a slight scrape on one side of her forehead from where she hit the ground.

"What have you been up to this evening? You smell like a brewery." She inspected her face. "Who did this to you, Belle?"

"Come on Momma. It's nothing. I..." She couldn't lie anymore. She broke down in her mother's arms and cried. "Why? Why am I like this? Why do I feel this way?" She looked into her mother's eyes. "Who am I?"

"Why, you're my daughter Belle."

"Who else's daughter? Who is my daddy?"

Chloe had to tell. She couldn't stand what it was doing to her daughter. She needed to free herself from this pain. She paused and then she began. "Your daddy was a black man. Well, I didn't know he was black. He was a mulatto, and because of his skin color, he was 'passing.'" Maybelle looked at her puzzled. "Someone who is black, but because they look white, they pass for being white."

"So, did he look like me?"

"Yes." She smiled. "You are the spitting image of him."

"So, what happened?"

"We met in New York. I was living in the Village at the time. I was at a coffee shop and he spotted me reading Dickinson.

"'Emily Dickinson, huh?'

"'Yes, she's been my favorite poet, ever since I was eight.'

"'I'm more of a transcendentalist, you know…Whitman, Longfellow, Emerson….'

"'Wow, I'm impressed. You really know your literature.'

"'I love it. May I join you?'

"Yeah, sure.' I chuckled at that."

"He asked, 'What's so funny?'

"'It's just you don't strike me as a guy who reads poetry or otherwise.'

"'Well, don't let this suit fool you. Why, if I had it my way, I would have been an English professor. But my father had other plans for me.'

"'Yeah, parents can really do that to you. Chloe Clemens. And you?" I extended my hand.'

"He took my hand and held it warmly. 'Julian. Julian Wright.' He looked at me so earnestly. 'You're so beautiful, Chloe. You're such a breath of newness. I noticed you when you walked in, and I said to myself, if I don't meet her, I will regret it for the rest of my life.'

"'You're too charming, Julian.'

"'I'm not trying to be, just truthful. I have to have you in my life.'

"'How can you tell by just this first meeting? I mean, we haven't even been on a date.'

"'Okay, consider this our first date.'

"We were inseparable after that. He took me home to meet his mother; however, she didn't seem too pleased to see me."

"'Hello, Mother. This is Chloe.'

"'Chloe. What a beautiful name. I was just about to sit down for tea, care to join me?'

"'Yes ma'am. I would love some.'

"'I detect an accent. Where are you from, dear?'

"'Mississippi.'

"'Really? That's funny—so am I'

"'Uhh....mother, how about that tea?'

"'Oh, yes. I'll go to the kitchen to see what's keeping her. Julian dear, would you join me?'

"'Well, mother I—.'

"'Dear, it wasn't a request.'

"'Of course.' To me, 'Would you excuse me?'

"'Of course. Hurry back.' He kissed me gently on the lips. I found out only later what had transpired in the kitchen."

"His mother said to him, 'So, you seem to be serious about this one.'

"'Mother, her name is Chloe, and yes, I am. I'm going to ask her to marry me, and I'd like your blessing, please.'

"'Julian, what would your father say if he were alive? God rest his miserable soul.'

"'I don't know? Go after what you want!'

"'Don't get smart with me, young man! You know he wouldn't approve of someone like her.

"'And what's wrong with Chloe?'

"'Who are her parents? What is her pedigree?'"

"'Gee, Mother. She's not a horse. What do I care.'

"'Just like your father. Don't care about the consequences.'

"'Okay, Mother. I'm not going to sit here and argue with you. I love that woman in there, and I'm going to marry her. You can cancel the tea.'

"'You need to think long and hard about what you're doing.'

"He hurried out of the kitchen.

"'Say hello to my former servant, if you decide to visit.'

He hesitated a bit, then continued toward the parlor.

"I knew something was wrong when he came from the kitchen. He took me by the hand and stormed out of his house.

"'Julian, wait! 'I pulled my hand out of his, which stopped him as well."

"'Chloe, marry me.'

"'What?'

"'Marry me. I want to start my life with you, and I don't want to wait any longer.'

"'Does this have anything to do with you and your mother talking in the kitchen?'

"'She's not...no, of course not. I want to marry you. Please say yes.'

"He looked so helpless. It seemed that if I were to turn him down, he would surely crumble before my eyes."

"'Yes. Of course.'

"We were married that afternoon. And a year later, we made our way to Mississippi to meet your grandma, grandpa, aunt, and uncle. Little did I know that the conversation he had with his mother that afternoon wasn't just a conversation at all."

"What do you mean?"

"Well, it turned out that he was actually from Mississippi and that his mother was a black woman and his father was white. He was raised by his father and his stepmother all of his life. Anyway, I was pregnant with you. I had one of those terrible headaches I sometimes get today, and we stopped at the pharmacy. I fell asleep. When I woke up, I saw him talking to a black woman."

"Who was she?"

"His sister."

"What happened?"

"Well, when he got back into the car, I questioned him about the woman."

"Did he tell you?"

"Not at first. He tried to lie, but then he realized he had to come clean."

"Then what happened?"

"What happened is what I will always regret. I ranted and raved about him being black and that he'd tricked me into marriage. I was so stupid. So blind and…"

"And what? What happened to my father?"

"They arrested him. And the next day, when I tried to get him out of jail, he was dead." Maybelle hesitated to ask but knew she needed to know. "How did he die?"

Chloe hesitated to reply but knew it was destined for her to know. "He was hung."

Maybelle looked at her mother confused, then disgusted. "You had him killed, didn't you?"

"Please, Belle. I didn't know…"

"That's why you're crazy. You killed my father. I didn't tell you, but one day, I went through your drawers and found a wedding picture of you and a man. Was that man my father?"

"Yes."

"So, I don't have a daddy because you're a fucking racist whore!"

Chloe slapped her daughter. "Don't you talk to me like that!"

"I hate you! I wish you were dead!"

"Well that makes two of us."

Maybelle stormed out of the room and slammed her bedroom door. Chloe was glued to the sofa. She couldn't move. She was frozen in the past. She recalled the day she cried, "Imposter!" and the morning when she found out her husband had been murdered. Tears welled in her eyes. She didn't have the heart to finish the story. She couldn't tell Maybelle that after her father was murdered, she'd tried to drown herself in the river with her inside, but was unsuccessful. Someone saw her body floating and rushed in to save her. All she needed was a few more minutes. When she recovered, she drove back to New York and had the baby. But all that didn't matter now because she was depressed. Too depressed to raise her daughter. So she gave up, and Maybelle grew up without a father *or* a mother.

Later that evening, Maybelle found her mother in the bathtub, bleeding out of her wrists. There was so much blood that it made puddles on the floor and turned the clear water red. In hysterics, she called the ambulance, and then her Auntie Roseanne, who rushed to see about her sister. Chloe knew, this time, her mother would surely die—but as fate had it….

While Chloe lay in the hospital, Roseanne suggested that she take Maybelle for a spell, while Chloe focused on getting better.

"Just for the summer, after school lets out. You should be better by then, and then she can come back here."

"It's not a magic pill that can make it all better. I'm never going to get better! I killed the only man I ever loved!"

"Stop it, Chloe! Just stop it! You gotta stop punishing yourself and forgive yourself. If not for you then for your daughter. She's in hysterics. You didn't see her. It took everything in me to calm her down. What have you done to her?"

Chloe offered no response.

"Okay, then it's settled. I will take Belle and you...well...you just..." her voice trailed.

"Okay. I...I'm so tired."

"I know you are. They're going to take good care of you here. You'll see. You'll walk out of here as good as new. You'll see." She rubbed her sister's coal black hair as she drifted off to sleep.

22

Maybelle lay in her bed. The morning light shone through the bedroom window. She had to see Tiger. She couldn't stay in that house any longer. She missed him. She really missed him. She'd stayed there while he walked away that afternoon. She stood there while he told her that it would never work. She was always a risk taker. She couldn't help herself. Then, her thoughts drifted to her mother. She wondered how she was doing. She wanted to call her but was paralyzed into inability to do so. She wanted to tell her that she was in love. Really this time. And all the other times were just pretend.

She also thought about how she got that Colored boy in a mound of trouble, almost getting him killed, and thrown in jail for rape. She wanted to tell her that, too. She should have told the policeman the truth, but she was so angry that she wanted all who dared to be around her to feel the pain she felt. She thought about her father and how she wished he was there to tell her what to do.

The more her thoughts ran, the angrier she became. She hated being in that deadbeat, racist town, and knew she didn't belong there or up North, or anywhere, for that matter. She wanted to tell Tiger the truth about her father, and the real reason why she was in Mississippi with her aunt and uncle, but she knew if she did, he would think she was trouble for sure and ruin what little chance she hoped to have with him. She was stuck—between love and pain. She was surely stuck.

That morning, she threw on a dress and shoes. She climbed down the vine-tree and cut across the field. She didn't know where she was going. She felt as if she were suffocating. She needed to escape. She ran and kept running until she couldn't. Her run turned to a slow trot and then a walk. She decided to go by the lake where the willow leaves brushed the water. Yes, that would do it for her. She had to think. She had to figure out what she was going to do about her mother. She didn't want to go back home, and she didn't want to stay with her aunt and uncle either. The only place was with Tiger, but now he didn't want her, or so it seemed.

As she got closer to her destination, she saw someone sitting there. It was him. She was so elated, but nervous. She didn't know if he would be happy to see her. She walked closer, and the closer she got, the slower her pace. He turned around and saw her standing there. He didn't say a word but walked toward her. They stood face to face, and before she could speak, he kissed her. She held on tight. They forgot their ill-fated barriers. He laid her down in the grass and kissed her more. He was free. She was free.

She unbuttoned his shirt. He rubbed his hand along her outer thigh. She rubbed his dark chest. He unbuttoned the white buttons that went down the front of her salmon-colored dress. She pushed him, slightly. He was startled. The top of her body became exposed as her dress opened, just enough for him to see her white bra and a bit of her white panties. She slowly pulled down the straps of her bra from her right shoulder, and then her left, and then down farther so that it was now around her waist.

Tiger looked at her full, white breasts and her pink nipples. She pulled his head down, and he began to kiss them and her neck and her lips. She moaned soft and low, surrendering to him to take her. And he did, under the willow tree that swung low, in the tall green grass, by the still lake, early that Saturday morning.

23

It was late afternoon when Maybelle and Tiger parted. They made plans to be with each other forever. To defy the laws of Crow. He made plans to meet her up North after he graduated. He urged her to be patient and told her that they would write each other. She said that she loved him and that she could never love anyone else more. He expressed the same and told her that he would be by her side soon. He told her to hold on and to take care of her mother. She expressed how hard it was but said that she would try. They kissed, and they parted.

Tiger decided to take the shortcut, a dirt road that led to his home. He knew he'd been out too long. His thoughts shifted to his father being home, and how good that felt. He trotted a bit faster when a car slowed up beside him. It was a sheriff's car. It was Sheriff Tanner, now up in age but still malignant as ever, more malicious than his father when he was sheriff. Like his father, J.T. did not tolerate out-of-line Negroes. He especially did not tolerate when races mixed, especially the black and white races. The car was going the pace of Tiger. Tiger slowed his trot but never stopped moving.

"What you into, boy?"

Tiger looked at the sheriff. His eyes were covered with a pair of shades. Tiger couldn't make out the situation because his eyes were covered. So, he just looked ahead and slowed his walk down a bit.

"Nothing," he said.

"Look like more than 'nothing.' Look like you was into something. Why, your shirt's untucked, you're sweaty…hmmm… look awful suspicious to me."

Tiger looked down at himself. He did look disheveled. He began to tuck in his shirt, and the car came to a screeching halt beside him.

"Like I said, what you been up to?"

"Nothing, sir. I was doing some work and now I'm done. I'm going home now."

"Unhm…what kinda work?"

"Just some outside work, but I'm going home now."

"Outside work...how 'bout I take you home?"

"No thanks. I live up the road. I can get home on my own."

"Well, I'm afraid that's not going to happen."

"Excuse me? Why are you stopping me, sheriff? I ain't done nothing."

"The hell you didn't. Someone said that they spotted a Negra raping a white girl, and you seem to fit that description."

"I didn't rape no one. I need to get home."

Tiger ran. The sheriff revved his engine and allowed Tiger to run a little ways before he came up beside him and hit him with his car. Tiger fell and rolled over on the dirt road. He was out. J.T. stopped his car and got out. He walked over to his unconscious prey to make sure he hadn't killed him—at least not like this, and not so soon. J.T. bent down and felt the pulse on the side of Tiger's neck. He dragged him and put him in the backseat of the police car. Tanner got in the driver's seat and looked in the rear-view mirror at his prize capture. This certainly brought back fond memories. A smile crept in the corners of his mouth as he drove off, excited at what the night would bring.

As evening fell, Tiger woke up in a holding cell at the small sheriff's station. A deputy sat at the desk and looked up from his paperwork, while Tiger stirred. When Tiger awoke, he felt pain on his side, and his leg was bruised.

"Hey, excuse me. I think I need a doctor. I'm banged up pretty bad."

The deputy said nothing but went back to whatever he'd been doing before he heard Tiger stirring.

"Hey! Sir. I need a doctor. I'm messed up pretty bad."

"I can't do nothing with you 'til the sheriff says otherwise."

"But I'm…." Tiger got up too fast, and he smarted all over. He winced, and his eyes began to well.

"I told you that I can't do nothing. You're brought in for raping a white girl."

"I don't know what you're talkin' about. I didn't rape a white girl….I…." His mind went back to him and Maybelle, making love in the grass. He knew they had been alone—at least he thought they were.

"Maybelle," he said under his breath.

"What's that you say?"

"I need to call my parents."

"The sheriff said that you're gonna have to wait to do that. Said he gotta figure out what to do with you."

"Do with me? What do you mean? Hey, I'm hurting and I need to talk to my parents, please."

Sheriff Tanner strutted out of nowhere with Mr. Simms trailing behind.

"Sheriff, why am I here? I didn't rape a white girl. I gotta talk to my parents, and I need a doctor."

"What you need, son, is a lesson learned, is what you need. You can't just go around, rapin' our women and not pay for it."

"Mr. Simms, I didn't rape Maybelle. We love each other. I wouldn't do anything to hurt her. Didn't she tell you? Didn't she tell you that, Mr. Simms?"

"There is nothing natural 'tween a Nigger and a white. I know you went against her will. I know it! We don't tolerate things like that in our family. We do what we can to get rid of the..." Simms looked at the sheriff, "undesirables." They both laughed.

"I know Maybelle didn't say that. Did you talk to her?"

They both laughed. "Boy, what you want, a press conference? Ain't no entertaining this any longer. Simms, you know what has to happen." He walked away and gave his deputy the eye. The deputy shot up and followed the sheriff.

"You won't get away with this, boy. I'm gonna personally make sure you pay for this, if it's the last thing I do on this Godforsaken earth."

"Mr. Simms, wait…Mr. Simms, please, don't do this!" Bill Simms stormed out of the station. Tiger stood there frozen. This was all too surreal. He couldn't believe that he was going to be one of those Coloreds who'd be punished for a crime he didn't commit.

>>>

"Where is Tiger? He should have been home hours ago."

"Did he tell you where he was going?"

"He told me he was going for a walk."

"A walk? Where? Why?"

Loretta was silent. She remembered the conversation between she and Tiger earlier that morning.

"Retta, where is he? Did he say where he was going?"

"He probably went to see that white girl. He said he'd be right back. I told him to be...." Loretta couldn't finish her sentence. She broke down and started to cry.

"I..." Ray felt what she was feeling. But instead of breaking down, he went straight to the hall closet.

Loretta looked at Ray despondently, "I have a feeling, Ray."

"Retta please...." Ray pulled out a black bag and packed some things in it. He, then pulled out his shotgun. The children came down the stairs.

"Daddy, what's going on? Where's Tiger?"

"Nothing, Terri, go back upstairs."

"Daddy, please. I'm not a kid. I know what's going on. Is he out seeing that white girl?"

"Terri, please."

"Mom, come on. You guys don't see what's going on? Tiger is in danger, and it's because you guys aren't paying attention."

"Terri, don't start." Ray cried.

"Don't start? Looks like things started a long time ago. Question is, how will it end?"

Both parents looked at the wise girl, standing before them, and then at each other.

Loretta sat on the loveseat and lay down on her side. "Truth is I think something's happened. It's that same feeling I got when you was stuck at that store and I told Tiger to fetch you... uhhh,Tiger!" She couldn't hold it together any longer.

"Retta, I said to stop it now! You can't go around talkin' this way. That's my boy. That's my boy." His voice cracked.

Loretta looked at him and noticed him falling apart. She walked over to where he stood with the shotgun in one hand and his free hand balled in a fist. She rubbed the side of his face. His cheek felt hard because his teeth were clinched. With tears in her eyes, "please find our son." And with that, she went upstairs and her children followed.

>>>

It was eight at night, and Tiger fell into a flaccid slumber on the floor of his cell. He heard the clank of the cell door open and unconsciously stirred. The deputy gave him a light kick on his foot.

"Get up."

"Am I going home?"

"Not exactly."

"Where am I going?

The deputy pulled him up from the floor.

"Where am I going? Where are my parents?"

"Put him in the back of the truck," a voice said. Tiger tried to see where the voice was coming from but was too groggy to distinguish it. When they arrived outside, the night air hit his face, which energized him a bit.

"Where are we going? What are you going to do with me?"

"You know, boy," Sheriff Tanner said, "you sure do ask a lot of questions. So, since you're so inquisitive, I'm gonna tell you what we're gonna do with you. We're gonna tie and gag you and put you in the back of this here pick-up and...well, I don't want to give away the whole surprise." His smile was a malicious one. He relished the prospect of what was to come.

24

Although he was only eight, J.T. knew much. However, what his mother told him that morning after would change his life forever. It went like this...

After T-Bone drove J.T. to the sheriff's office for questioning, he drove him to the hospital to see his mother. She was banged up pretty bad. J.T. sat in the chair next to the bed. He reached out his fat little hand to put it in hers. He lifted her hand to his cheek, and the tears began to flow. When she felt the wetness on her skin, she slowly and carefully opened her eyes. She managed a half-smile and took the hand her beloved son was holding to caress his soft, curly brown hair.

The sting in her voice made it hard for her to speak. And the bruises on her lips made it even harder for her to form her words. However, she knew she needed to talk to her son. She needed to tell him the truth before she died. She was dying. The beating she'd gotten the night before had been meant to kill her. He'd wanted to kill her. He wanted her to feel the same pain that she'd caused him for eight years. So he beat her and slammed her and bashed her head against the wall three times and threw her on the floor. He stood in the middle of the floor and cried. He couldn't believe that J.T. belonged to a Nigger and not to him.

"What the hell is wrong with you, you evil, evil woman? How-could-you-hu-mi-li-ate-me?!" With every syllable, the kicks grew harder, until she doubled over and began spitting up the food from earlier, along with blood. She wheezed, she gagged, and she coughed.

"I...I'm so sor..."

"You don't get to talk! You don't get to say anything! You got me raisin' a Nigger boy, you Nigger-lovin' bitch!"

"Tanner, please. I never meant to hur--."

He bent down to where she lay and yanked her hair back so he could see her face.

"Well you did. You did hurt me. And now I gotta tell that Nigger boy that he ain't mine."

His voice was low, and foam formed in the corners of his mouth. He slapped her, and her head hit the floor. He was hysterical, and she knew it was either him or her. She eased her body toward the bed. His hands covered his face while he cried. She took this opportunity to feel underneath the mattress, where the springs held the knife she had hidden in case this day came. She felt and rummaged until she was able to grab the handle of the knife. Slowly, she eased the knife out of its hiding place and placed it behind her back. Just when she thought she was successful, he turned around to witness her act of insurgency.

"What is that?"

"Tanner, no."

He rushed over to find the knife in her left hand. He bent her arm all the way back until it popped like a twig.

"Uuuuaaaaahh." The scream was blood curdling. The pain was so severe that she passed out. Just as he rose to get his footing, he stumbled and fell forward onto the knife she held in her hand. He couldn't scream. He was more in shock than he was hurt. He rose to his feet and stumbled toward the other side of the room, hit the wall, and slid down onto the floor.

J.T. walked out of the hospital room in a daze. He could not believe that the man he had killed was not his father. He could not think anymore. He needed some relief. He needed to get away from all things human. He decided to go fishing. When he walked out of the hospital, T-Bone was waiting for him in the truck.

"You knew about this?"

"Knew about what?"

"That I am the son of a Nigger."

T-Bone was quiet. He couldn't believe that his sister had told. He didn't have the heart to tell him the truth. That his mother had an affair with the sharecropper up the road. That he would come around every now and again to fix things around the house, while Tanner was at work. When she got wind of her pregnancy, she stopped the affair immediately. However, she was afraid of the outcome, so she told her brother and swore him not to tell.

"What if that baby come out dark? Then whatcha gonna do?"

"I don't know? I just hope that he ain't."

Fortunately, she was saved with the exception of some features; however, it was all brushed off with talk of genes from long ago. Some rumors formed that the boy wasn't the sheriff's but belonged to the Colored sharecropper up the road. Those rumors were quashed quickly after the sheriff became violent and irate. But one day, the boy came home from fishing all day with his friends and when he walked in the house, he was brown as toast. The sheriff knew and became angry. That's when the beatings began.

"I'm sorry, J.T..I--."

"Where is he?"

"Uh...dead."

J.T. stared at T-Bone. "How?"

"Your daddy killed him. When he suspected it, he hung 'im high."

"So, I don't have a daddy?"

"No son. I'm sorry."

"Just as well." J.T. sunk down even farther in his seat. His thoughts wandered to the conversation he'd had with the deputy earlier, before seeing his mother for the last time.

>>>

"Look, J.T., I know you took the handle. I saw you give it to T-Bone, while y'all was in the kitchen."

"I..."

"Hey, I don't give a damn about that. I hated the sumbitch anyway, but I respected what he did. No offense I hope."

"Yeah...why?"

"Why, what?"

"Why did you respect him if you hated him so much?"

"Because your pop knew the law. He knew how to do things, how to get things.

He was very resourceful, and he taught me a lot. Tanner was a damned good sheriff.

"Yeah, well the only thing I learned from that bastard was how to hit a woman real good. I hated him too."

"Don't speak ill of the dead. Besides, she had it comin'."

J.T. rose from out of his chair. "Don't you talk about my momma like that."

"I'm sorry, son. You're right. No woman deserves that kinda beatin' on the regular. It's bound to kill...well...no one deserves to be mistreated."

"She's gonna die, ain't she?"

"I reckon she might."

"What am I gonna do?"

"You got T-Bone."

"No offense, but T-Bone can't nurse a cold, let alone raise a kid."

"Well, you ain't got no one else. So you don't have a choice."

"You ain't got no kids. Why don't you raise me the rest of the way?"

"Look Jessie, you're a good kid and all, but..."

"Then it's settled. You're gonna raise me 'til I can fend for myself."

The deputy leaned back in his chair that swiveled. He gazed at J.T. long and hard. His eyes narrowed, and then he spoke. "You sure you want this?"

"I've never been more sure of anything."

"Okay, since I'm the successor of your daddy, I'll teach you everything that he taught me about the law and how it's done in the South. You'll be raised in this here station, and when the time is right, you'll sit right here in this chair. I've always admired you, Jessie Tanner. You're gonna be a force to be reckoned with when the time is right."

J.T. stood up and walked out of the already-propped-open door. He walked toward the truck, opened the door, and sat on the passenger side. He leaned back in the seat. He thought about the conversation that had just transpired between him and his now-guardian, the sheriff. Knowing that he had tainted blood running through his veins sickened him. He leaned over and put his head between his legs. T-Bone looked at him befuddled. He ached to know what conversation had taken place between those two but decided to question later.

J.T. stayed like that for a minute but then rose up like a new person. He now had purpose, to kill and destroy those like his biological father. As far as he was concerned, a Nigger made him kill his father. A Nigger made his father kill his mother. A Nigger made him an orphan. A Nigger destroyed his family. And for that, they would have to pay. Yes, and being sheriff someday would be just the ticket.

"J.T., you all right?"

"I'm fine. Now, take me to see my momma so's I can go fishing."

25

Tiger tried to fight his way loose. The deputy's leviathan grip became more constricted, but something in Tiger pushed him to fight even harder—that thing inside him—that same thing that had caused the meaning of his name to come to fruition. He fought, but just when the hold the deputy had on him weakened, Tiger was hit with a blow to the back of the head, which knocked him to the ground.

"You're late." Sheriff Tanner said to the one who'd struck Tiger.

"Sorry, Jessie. It was hard for me to get away tonight. The missus was drivin' me crazy 'bout being out the third night this week." He looked at him a bit agitated.

"I don't wanna hear about your damn whiny wife. I got a job to do here, and by golly I'm gonna see it through."

"Damn it, Jessie. What are we doing here? You gotta stop doin' this. I mean, I don't like the Niggers no more'n you, but for crying out loud, this gotta stop!!"

"Don't you dare talk to me that way." He spat those words out so maliciously that his face turned redder than a pepper. "I could crush you. I could destroy you. Do you know who I am?!" Sheriff Tanner exploded but then collected himself. "So if we have families to get to, that means that we have to get this thing done quickly, hey boys? Now, Simms wants justice for the rape of his niece, so that's what we'll do. Get a rope and catch this Negra by the toe. Gag his mouth, too."

"So where are we going this time, Sheriff?" the deputy asked.

"Hmm, down by the lake where he took advantage of her. That'll teach him to mess around with our women."

Tiger was out cold from the blow to the back of the head. The ride was bumpy, causing Tiger's head to knock against the side of the truck from the inside. He went in and out of consciousness. "Maybelle..." he mumbled over and over. When the truck stopped, the three men immediately got out and opened the door to the bed of the truck. Tiger was tied up like a hog, with his hands and feet together. The man dragged him out of the truck. Tiger fell to the ground with a *thud*. He could be heard through his gag, moaning and smarting.

"Say, did this kid really rape this girl? I mean, what do we really know about this? She's from up north, for crying out loud, a Yank. What do you care about a Yank?" said the deputy.

"Simms is my friend. Hell, a similar thing happened to his sister-in-law almost twenty years ago, and I took care of that like I'm takin' care of this. These Negras are slick. They're dirty, filthy, sexual varmints that deserve to die. I hate 'em."

"Of course, I was there, remember?"

"Hardly." Tanner snorted.

"Well, I've seen him around, and he just don't seem like...he's an all right kid. He don't cause no trouble around and..."

"What's wrong with you, boy?" Tanner barked.

"Look sheriff, I thought we was gonna scare him a little—you know, make him cry and all. I didn't know we was gonna murder him. Besides, we don't even know if these allegations are true. For all we know that girl could be makin' up the whole thing."

"Look, you bastard...." The deputy became uneasy, observing the abhorrent glare in Tanner's eye. "I don't have time to go word for word with you over some damn coon. Now get that boy and drag him to that tree over there, and let's get this whole debacle over and done."

The man who owned the truck grabbed some rope and gasoline. The deputy dragged Tiger's body over to the tree nearest to the lake. He really couldn't see what he was doing because it was pitch black, save for the headlights from the truck. While he dragged Tiger's body, his thoughts streamed to long ago to when he was in the car with Simms's sister-in-law, explaining to her about what had happened to her husband. He became distracted and stumbled over a large root from a tree that stuck out from the ground. He fell backward and hit his head on the boulder. Tiger's body fell on top of him.

"What in tarnation? Boy, what you done did?" Tanner shouted. He got closer to the deputy and saw that he was out cold. "Ah, hell. Rob, grab that boy and string 'im up. We'll deal with that good for nothing, later."

Rob pulled Tiger off the deputy.

"Useless piece of... I don't know why I keep you on."

The deputy didn't know either. He'd been doing this for about twenty years now. Although the job had its perks, the random lynchings that occurred were the worst, and it took everything in him not to quit and go back home. He knew, though, that after all these years, he was in too deep. So he became numb...to everything.

Rob tied the noose around Tiger's neck, and before he hung him high, Tiger came to. He felt the noose around his neck and screamed through his gag. Rob beat Tiger mercilessly. He needed him to be unconscious for his personal preference. He hated when they looked at him, so he'd smash their eyes with his fist. And sometimes, the gag would fall, so he'd punch their mouths and knock their teeth out. And then, he felt a little guilt and wondered if he'd want to recognize his kid if he were in this position, so he decided to beat them until they were unrecognizable to any human eye.

This was normally the "fun" part, but with the deputy out of commission and Frank, the other one who would normally accompany Rob, out of town, it was just him and the sheriff—and the sheriff was acting like a real jerk tonight. He didn't understand that this was the third night this week some coon was being hung. Of course he loved a good hangin', was part of some real good ones back in the day, but now he was getting up in age and couldn't do these things anymore. His new wife was a devout Christian, and if he wanted to make this marriage work, he had to be good. So he begged and pleaded with her and told her that this was the last night that he'd be out, and for her not to wait up.

"All right, you beat him enough. I think you like that part, you sick bastard." Tanner laughed a big, hearty laugh. "Jeeze, I guess the deputy's useless. Come on, let's get this coon off his feet.

Rob grabbed Tiger and put him on his feet. He was an old pro. The entire ritual was natural to him, for both men for that matter, like breathing. Rob swung the remaining rope over the thick tree branch and pulled, and pulled, and pulled. Tiger squirmed like a fish out of water. His feet dangled and jerked the more Rob pulled. The veins in his neck bulged, and tears streamed from his eyes. His screams were caught by every pull— staccato— fragmented. Rob tied the remaining rope around a neighboring tree.

Tiger knew he was going to die. He knew that there was no one to save him. He thought about all the people who mattered to him the most...and then, his body went limp. Rob threw gasoline on

Tiger, but before he could strike the match and toss it on the victim, headlights shone from a vehicle driving toward the scene.

"Tanner, wait!" Simms jumped out of his truck.

"Well, well…changed your mind, huh? I understand. There's nothing like a good old-fashioned lynching. So good, you just can't stay away."

"No, this is wrong. I can't let you do this." He walked closer to Tiger. "Jesus, what have you done?"

"Our jobs. Now, unless you're feeling nostalgic, leave us be so justice can be served.

"Please, Tanner. I can't let you do this, and I won't be a party to it anymore. What we did with that boy almost twenty years ago… I still have nightmares. I was just angry. Maybelle loves that boy. She cried to me almost an hour, trying to convince me not to hurt him. Besides, I already drove one Clemens girl crazy. I can't do it again. You know, Tanner, this is only the repeat of history, and I just can't stomach it any longer. I'm too old and way too regretful."

He turned on his flashlight and looked at Tiger from head to toe, hanging from the tree. "Is that boy dead?" He turned to Tanner, "Just cut 'im down and I'll take him to a hospital. I won't tell anyone about this. Just let 'im go."

Tanner looked at Simms with suspicion and disappointment.

"Come on, Simms, you went and gone soft on me? Besides, what's one more dead Nigger anyhow? Ain't nobody gonna miss this boy. Nobody that matters, anyhow."

Simms stared at his longtime friend of almost thirty years.

Tanner motioned to Rob to cut Tiger down. Rob took the knife out of his pocket and cut Tiger down. He fell limp to the ground. Tiger was still unconscious. Simms bent down and touched Tiger's neck to feel for a pulse.

"Hmm, still alive. He's a fighter." He looked up at the sheriff. "Thank you, Jessie. I can take it from here."

"No, I'll take care of the boy. Besides, it'll come out better coming from me." Bill hesitated a bit. "Sure, I guess." He turned to walk away. "Hey, you sure you got this? I'd be more than...."

"I'll call you to let you know how everything turned out, hear?"

"Okay." Simms walked away, got in his truck, and drove off.

Sheriff Tanner bent down next to Tiger, who was now conscious in a fetal position, still gagged and bound. He took out his flashlight so he could see where the blood was oozing out over his eyebrow. "You really think I'm gonna let you go? Now, you may have escaped the death of a lynching, but you're still gonna die."

Tiger screamed through his gag.

"Rob, light that stick up for me so's I can set fire to this Nigger."

Rob wrapped a rag around the wooden stick, poured gasoline on it, and set fire to it. While he watched the fire illuminate the darkness, he handed it to Tanner. Tanner held the fire, wooden stick to Tiger's face. All that showed in the light from the flames was Tiger's battered face and the whites of his eyes. He screamed and cried through the gag.

Tanner got down on one knee and whispered in Tiger's ear. "Rot in hell, you sonofabitch."

Tanner set fire to Tiger. Tiger screamed and pleaded....

"Get that damn deputy and put him in the truck. I'm gettin' rid of his ass, first thing."

Rob walked over to where the deputy was still out cold, picked him up with one arm, and dropped him over his shoulder. The two men walked back to the truck. As the men drove off the dirt road and onto the street, another truck was driving in the opposite direction. The person in the truck spotted the flames in the distance and drove toward it...

Tonight, Tiger was in the clutches of hell, and its origin was the devil.

THE END

About the Author:

Wanda Coppedge is from Washington, DC and has served as an English instructor for over 17 years in the public and private sectors as well as a lecturer at Howard University and Maryland University. She's earned her degree in Theater Arts at the University of the District of Columbia. After graduating, she ventured into an acting career in the theatre for 10 years. After much resistance, she chose a career of teaching high school English and has not stopped since.

One thing that has not changed is her passion for writing. She has written articles for the Online DC Examiner, advocating for our youth in the educational arena. Now she has embarked on another career as a novelist. Her work takes on provocative real life issues and turns them into unpredictable fiction. She especially loves delving into the veracity of a character, understanding that everyone has his or her reasons for being the way he or she is, and explores those reasons in a raw and candid manner.

Wanda's life has been full. She has been blessed in doing everything she has set her heart and mind to do, and is still going. She aspires for her body of work to become classics to be enjoyed in the classrooms and beyond, for years to come.

Wanda has two wonderful daughters and resides in Washington, DC.

www.ingramcontent.com/pod-product-compliance
Lightning Source LLC
Chambersburg PA
CBHW050343190726
48284CB00007BB/2122